NO PEACE AT VERSAILLES

AND OTHER STORIES

NINA BARRAGAN

Minnesota Voices Project Number 43

New Rivers Press 1991

Copyright © 1991 by Nina Barragan
Library of Congress Catalog Card Number 90-61085
ISBN 0-89823-123-x
All Rights Reserved
Edited by C. W. Truesdale
Cover painting by Alan Weinstein
Book Design by Gaylord Schanilec
Data entry by Samuel Pickering
Typesetting by Peregrine Publications

Two of the stories in *No Peace at Versailles and Other Stories* have previously appeared in earlier versions in these publications: *The Long Story* and *Revista/Review Interamericana*. Our thanks to the editors for allowing us to reprint these stories here.

Publication of *No Peace at Versailles and Other Stories* has been made possible by grant support from the Jerome Foundation, the Arts Development Fund of the United Arts Council, the Beverly J. and John A. Rollwagen Fund of the Minneapolis Foundation, Cray Research Foundation, the Elizabeth A. Hale Fund of the Minneapolis Foundation, the First Bank System Foundation, Liberty State Bank, the Star Tribune/Cowles Media Company, the Tennant Company Foundation, the Valspar Corporation, and the National Endowment for the Arts (with funds appropriated by the Congress of the United States). New Rivers Press also wishes to acknowledge the Minnesota Non-Profits Assistance Fund for its invaluable support.

New Rivers Press books are distributed by

The Talman Company
150-5th Avenue
New York, NY 10011

Bookslinger
2402 University Avenue
St. Paul, MN 55114

No Peace at Versailles and Other Stories has been manufactured in the United States of America for New Rivers Press (C. W. Truesdale, Editor/Publisher), 420 N. 5th Street/Suite 910, Minneapolis, MN 55401 in a first edition of 1,200 copies.

*To my mother Emilia Barragan Lasansky
and to my father Mauricio Lasansky
for giving me wings*

*To my husband Alan Weinstein
for believing I could fly*

CONTENTS

   1 Whatever Became of Robin Bender?
 13 Son
 22 Livia and the Gypsies
 28 Five White Shirts
 40 Friends of the Teatro Colón
 50 No Peace at Versailles
 64 The Mechanics of Turbulence in Fluid
 76 A Gentle Madness
 82 Lilly and Bruno
 92 The Napoleonic Wars
102 The Swimmer from Vanishing Point
119 Conversation in the Late Afternoon
123 Wasn't Hemingway at Enghien?

WHATEVER BECAME OF ROBIN BENDER?

"It had neither entrance nor exit, and its most remarkable feature was the curious maze of screened, summer porches that clung like vines. It was the strangest building," Robin said thoughtfully, glancing across the breakfast table at her husband. "Wooden and many storied, it looked like a cross between an old summer cottage, dozing over a lake, and a cartoonish interpretation of the tower of Babel. I'm sure it's supposed to mean something, a structure without a door." Robin paused, waiting, but Bernard continued eating his grapefruit silently.

She shrugged lightly. "We stood in front of it for the longest time, and I kept checking the address in my purse, but it was correct. You told me you would wait for me in the McDonald's Hamburg place across the street from it."

Bernard looked up, Robin continued talking. She did not want her husband to interrupt. "It's alright, I understood," she said, closing her eyes momentarily. "I realized I had to go alone, and that it would not be easy, but I was anxious to deliver the long overdue gift. It was small and wrapped in white tissue paper, with a blue cord. I couldn't remember exactly what — only that it was a fragment of some kind.

"The climb was awful and strenuous. I was gripped by the frustrating sensation of making no progress. Scaling the side of the structure and dangerously jumping from porch to porch, I hoped to find some loosened screens that would permit my entry. I kept looking back over my shoulder to see you, Bernard. At some point I was suddenly holding onto a doll." Robin smiled, "You know how dreams are always throwing you a curve, just to complicate things, well it was Marla's doll, and it was making my climb even more difficult. I decided to let it drop to a tree branch where it could be recovered once I was down again. Finally locating some opened windows within a porch, I climbed inside and found myself in a large room with a group of preschool children. I asked them if they knew where the Democratic Party Headquarters were. They told me it was up three flights of stairs and to my right.

"Upstairs, there was no one out in the hall so I opened the large door and entered. The room was in total darkness. I groped along the wall searching for a light switch.

"'Would you please turn off the light and close the door. There's a meeting in progress!'

"Approximately ten men sat around an oval table smoking cigars and talking. Several other people stood about waving flags and wearing political caucus hats. They made me so nervous I immediately reached for the light switch just as a short, stout man stood up from the table and hurried towards me. Do you know who it was?" Robin asked, leaning across the table towards Bernard. "Charles Humphrey, my thesis advisor. But I don't think he was the same person." She paused, her voice perplexed, "He'd become loud and self-confident." She had a sip of her coffee. "Mind you, he looked the same, bloodshot eyes, sweaty forehead, thinning hair. He wore that flat, straw-like hat pushed to the back of his head. I haven't seen him in years, not since my dissertation, but do you know that just the other day I talked to him on the phone? Anyway he grabbed me by the elbow and led me out to the hall.

"'What are you doing here, Robin, I thought you were apolitical.'

"His voice was rough and aggressive, as though he hadn't time, as though he'd become very much in demand. I told him we wanted to make a contribution to the Democratic Party.

"'Great!' he said, holding out his hand eagerly.

"Carefully I handed him the small, white tissue paper package.

"'What the hell is this?!'"

Robin shook her head at Bernard. "Remember how mild-mannered he was? I never heard him swear. I told him I was pretty sure it was a fragment of Paracas embroidery, and that I got it when I was in –

"'Shit Robin,' he said, "I don't believe this."

"That was it? You woke up?" Bernard asked incredulously, pushing aside his grapefruit half.

Robin nodded calmly, her fingers playing with her coffee mug. She felt slightly relieved to have told him about the dream, but now he was going to say something nasty.

"It must have felt pretty anti-climactic, after that climb!" Bernard snickered sarcastically as he reached for the butter and jam and carefully centered a piece of toast on his plate.

Robin stared at him as though he had suddenly turned to wax. The self-confident snicker still managed to offend her. It was amazing, after all these years. Her mother used to accuse her of being too generous with him, too willing to forgive. Perhaps she'd been right. But Robin loved him, she always had, and she understood he would probably never outgrow his smallness, his meanness. A quick, effortless fact, she realized, somewhat shocked. A bright light of honesty in a recently graying mind. Robin stole a fast guilty look across the table. As usual, he was immaculate; his hair, the starched pale blue shirt, his white fingertips. Years ago, when Bernard had learned, horrified, that she had stood in dusty sandals taking part in the unwrapping of a mummy bundle in Peru, he'd become so upset he could hardly contain himself. Those long shrouds of linen were no doubt harboring everything from leprosy to leukemia, he insisted, disgusted and impatient. "Why mummy bundles for your Ph.D., and why Peru?" he had blurted angrily, only weeks before their pending wedding. Robin understood that he was really asking why fate would have him fall in love with her. She had no answer for that, so she tried to explain how breathtakingly beautiful the Paracas textiles were – the tireless weavings, yards and yards, the elaborate embroideries. He refused to be moved, and spoke only of how she had stood there breathing in the diseased dust of the Incas.

'Paracas,' she had corrected him.

'Whatever, it's two thousand-year-old dust, for God's sake! What are you going to pass on to our children?'

She re-focused on Bernard's toast, on his hands.

'Magical fingers' his mother had announced, when her son, Dr. Bernard Bender, had been made Chief of Surgery.

But what of his eyes? Robin had often wondered exactly what it was he saw, what he was capable of seeing, and what he permitted. Or were eyes his only accessories to his work, his surgery? But surely there he had depth of perception, the ability to distinguish between hue and shade, the desire for visual refinement. She did wonder, though, for he had never cared to make visual decisions about anything except his clothes and his cars. She'd always suspected that he lacked an aesthetic hot line running from the eyes to the gut. Not that it was unusual. She had come to understand that the lives of many people were not motivated by visuality. Sometimes she found it absolutely amazing that she had shared the greater part of her life with this man.

"It was a frustrating dream," Robin said, shaking the hair from her face, the enervating thoughts from her mind. If only she had passed on some of that Paracas dust to her daughters, those two beautiful, blond aliens who sometimes occupy her house. They wear sweat bands and beautiful jogging suits early in the mornings. And then they change, skirts. And they change, shorts for after school. And they change, jeans for the evening play rehearsals. Robin envisioned the horror on their faces, should it be decreed throughout the land that only lengths of fine linen were to be wrapped around the unpainted, female body.

She leaned across the table with the intent to re-focus; to be willing, to be wifely. She watched as Bernard methodically buttered his toast. Despite his compulsion, she promised not to turn him to wax again that morning. "Do you suppose I chose the Democratic Party because I thought it represented something important, something I was willing to climb for?"

Bernard shrugged, biting carefully into his toast. "Could be. But a fragment, why would anyone give a fragment as a campaign contribution? Honestly, Robin." Bernard shook his head impatiently and swallowed some coffee. "If I were Humphrey, I'd be swearing too."

"It was wrapped before my dream started," Robin said defensively. She was not surprised that Bernard would try to make her feel incompetent in her dreams as well. "I didn't even get to see it," she complained, pouring herself some more coffee. "And I wish I had, they're so hard to come by now, and the dealers are asking outrageous prices. Bernard," Robin's voice became quiet and thoughtful, "what if it was valuable? What if they could have sold it?"

"I doubt it," Bernard said firmly, humorlessly, as he finished off his toast.

"I suppose the idea of giving a fragment came from those shards of ancient pottery I had kicking around the house for years." Robin smiled. "Remember, I got them through a dealer in Peru?"

"Robin, that was before we were married. You always expect me to remember the strangest things."

Robin turned away and stared out the kitchen window. She could see the branches moving in the April wind, but the sun was out, and the weather report had promised a bright, crisp day. The girls had their jazz dance class and she had ballet in an hour. Perhaps she should suggest they all walk. No, her daughters would never agree, Robin decided. Somedays her sense of isolation was enormous.

Perhaps Charles Humphrey was right. He'd called from the University two days ago, asking her to come and teach one of his seminars. She'd hemmed and hawed, and just as last year when he'd called, she'd finally said no, coming up with the same excuse about not being ready to handle the responsibility. He became silent, but she knew he was angry. Why didn't he shout and call her a coward! Why didn't he swear and say that if she was willing to let her husband treat her the way he did, that was her business, but she had no right acting as though scads of research had already been done — which of course wasn't so — she had no right letting her mind turn to mush. Why didn't he rant and rave? But no, in silent exasperation, he had finally hung up, saying that she clearly seemed not to know what she wanted, and *he* certainly didn't. Poor Charles, he must have worked up a terrible sweat on his forehead, Robin realized, thinking of his control, his silence, as he sat at his chaotic desk. She thought perhaps she liked him better in her dream, swearing and aggressive.

She turned back to Bernard. "Do you think my dropping the doll means I've had to do that in my life, leave something important behind? Dreams are supposed to be loaded with symbolism."

"Robin, why do you always have to make something out of nothing?"

She shrugged. "I haven't had such a strange dream in years." Her voice was quiet. "Do you remember about ten years ago I dreamt my grandfather died?"

"No."

"Don't you? The next day we heard your cousin was dead."

"So, no one died in this dream."

"I know, but I have a sense of foreboding about it."

Bernard shook his head impatiently. "I've got to run," he said, glancing at his watch. He wiped his mouth and stood up.

"Dance classes this morning?" he asked, standing erect and trim, holding on to the back of his chair, looking down at her.

Robin nodded self-consciously, slouching deeper in her chair. He didn't enjoy waking up to her anymore. She watched him leave the kitchen and walk down the hall towards the front entrance. Her hair wasn't up to much before ten, and the most that could be said for her bathrobe was that it was warm. She heard him open the front closet and put on his coat. As for her figure, that was why she was taking dance. She had determined to pull herself into shape. She heard his 'see you later,' and then the front door. But figure or no figure, she was still Robin. She was still Robin! There had been times, while making love, when Bernard would sit on the edge of the bed. She'd seen stars; bright, beautiful stars. Under the influence of stars, anything was possible.

The old Women's Gym was like a Carnegie library, clean and still and solid. Institutional 1930s oak benches occupied the wainscotted lobby and hallways, and two dreary, sanitary bathrooms flanked the main staircase. In the large dance studio, the sun's rays entered the old, high windows, combining with the hot water radiators to create a pleasant, time warp warmth. When Robin had recently realized that more often than not her right hand was clenched into a tight fist, she opted for ballet, hoping for some organized exercise and relaxation. She had never considered herself tense, but was it possible that now, at 45, she was becoming so? There were ten of them at the barre, fumbling through their *pliés* and *tendues*, blotches of bright, leotard colors in the far wall mirrors. It wasn't bad from a distance. But when the young instructor, Sarah, called them to the center of the room to stand before the mirror, face on in neat rows of fives, that was bad.

Very bad, Robin realized. Reality, reality. She admitted to the gentle pads of hip fat, and the flabby stomach muscles – they were both repairable, both within her power – but what about time's overall squaring off? Having lost the light, graceful swing of youth, the breasts appeared mass-like in the leotard. Her neck had definitely shortened over the years, and the settled jawline was the undeniable giveaway. It was her own fault. She could have joined an aerobics course for women her own age, but no, she had to register for Beginning Ballet. The fact that it was held Saturday morning and was part of the University's extension program, hadn't made things easier. The other bodies in the mirror might not be more graceful, but they were still in their early twenties. She should have listened to her daughters.

"Ballet?! Well then I'm taking jazz dance!" Margot said firmly, cutting up the tomato.

Robin removed the roast from the oven, ignoring her eldest daughter's remark.

"Marla, did you hear?"

Marla had just entered the kitchen with an empty glass.

"Mom's registering for ballet!" Long-suffering, Margot ungracefully scraped the board of tomatoes into the salad.

"I don't believe it!" Marla turned, watching as Robin lifted the roast onto the platter. "Mother, is this some kind of joke?"

"What?"

"Are you really going to take ballet?"

"Sure, why not?"

"Aren't you going to feel just a little out of place?" Marla waited for a response from her mother. "You know what I mean," she said, staring at the roast. After a few seconds she looked up. "They have an adult exercise class, why don't you take that instead?" Her voice was hopeful.

"Because I want to take ballet."

"Come on Mom, be serious!"

"About what?"

"Forget it!" Marla sighed, leaving the kitchen.

"Tummy in, leg straight, head erect."

Sarah gently touched shoulders, tapped arms and straightened feet as she walked down the line, supervising the *dégagés*. Her own punky, cropped hair hung into pretty, large eyes, despite her insistence that hair must be pulled back. She had a wonderful, long body, though perhaps a little too much bosom for a dancer. But she was a dancer, determined, hard-working, and mostly exhausted. When they'd arrived for class that morning, they'd found her sitting on the floor with scissors and layers of wrapping. Dancers were forever constricting or liberating parts of their bodies. In this case, one leg seemed to wear more than the other. An extra winding of gray stuff peeked out from under the black legging she had cut off mid-calf. There were white cotton socks with their toes cut out, leg warmers, and a leotard with its sleeves removed. At the joints of visible flesh – hands, elbows, one ankle – her skin was scraped and sore and cold-looking, as though she were an abused child, with lousy circulation. Robin hoped dancers were kinder to their souls than they were to their bodies.

Sarah waited for a beat, concentrating, frowning. "The record is not right," she announced, perturbed, "I'll have to find something else." She threw on her sweater and breezed towards the door.

She was kind to persevere, kind to ignore the fact that they were not especially agile, and some were downright awkward.

Left alone, several of the students slumped to the floor in an exhausted heap, others stood about talking. Robin remained in position at the barre, bending and reaching first to her right, then to her left. She would stretch and exercise, she would not slacken, she would not think about her dream and that strange building, or Bernard, or the constricting grasp of middle age. While she did not care to admit it, the truth was, youth had been better.

"Last week you told me you lived in Peru for a time?"

Robin turned to the voice beside her. The law major had her left leg on the barre, her torso bent over it like a softened, pink crayola.

"I spent a year in Lima when I was doing research for my Ph.D."

"That must have been awhile back. Was it nice then?"

"Beautiful." Robin added, hoisting her leg – not without effort – up onto the barre, ignoring the part about awhile back.

"Last summer I traveled around South America with a few friends," the girl said. "We were in Lima for a few days, but there was dog shit all over the sidewalks." She lowered her leg and turned, lifting her right leg onto the barre.

"Again?"

"I haven't done this side yet," the girl explained.

"I mean the dog problem," Robin said. "It was like that when I was there, but then I heard they kicked the hippies out of the main square, and that they were trying to pass dog ordinances."

The law major shrugged and lowered her leg.

In Lima, Robin had worked with a lanky Dutch ethnologist. Equally committed to Paracas research, they were drawn together by an overwhelming passion for the remarkable weavings and embroideries, relishing the unbelievable excitement of discovery. She had never forgotten how his placid countenance and rather plain flat face underwent an extraordinary transformation as he prepared to examine a piece of weaving. He became agitated and pale. Tiny muscles began to undulate around his mouth as he noisily sucked in air and nervously wiped his glasses and then his damp hands with a handkerchief. When his tall frame finally leaned over the ancient garment, an awesome unity of eye, mind, and spirit took hold; his calm returned, and he gently, lovingly observed every inch. One windy day in spring, they left their work, took a picnic, and drove out to the ocean in a tiny car. His folded legs and bony knees occupied most of the front seat space as they spoke about their research in an excited mixture of English and Spanish. Later, while they ate and stared out at the ocean, he told her about the sand dunes on the North Sea, near his home. She told him about Central Park. Then, because it was not sunny and because there was not a soul around, they quickly made love – never having touched before – yet hoping to form bonds that would separate them from the North Sea and Central Park.

Sarah was back, the record in place, the rond de jambes in motion along the barre.

"You must be sure to use *these* muscles," Sarah said, patting her butt, as she demonstrated in the middle of the dance studio. She did several rond de jambes. "The muscles in your –" she hesitated, "here," she patted her behind again. "Your popo!" "Tighten your popo!"

Robin was struck with such amazement, she nearly burst out in hysterical laughter. Popo? Sarah was so comfortable with her body, she didn't mind the world knowing its intricasies: the alluring dip of her lower back, the shape and hang of her breasts, and her loosely hinged hips, her terrific turnout. And yet, she couldn't bring herself to say butt, or ass, or rear end. So she talked about popo. Robin understood about Sarah's sense of liberation, but she did wonder about the underlying sources of prudishness.

Ten minutes left of class, and Robin was tired of holding in her stomach. She wondered how the girls were doing. Jazz dance was far more strenuous. They'd be fine. Like Bernard, they both had a tremendous amount of nervous energy. And like Bernard, they had the self-confidence to convince themselves of almost anything, even the impossible and ridiculous. Robin often wished she had that ability. Since the age of their enlightenment, the girls had maintained a bottom line belief that their generation had invented equality, sex, and groovy clothes. Robin smiled. What would they think if they knew that back in the early sixties, their mother had made 'free love,' and that she'd inadvertantly been a trend-setter, sporting denim skirts, leather thongs, and a single, long braid, while others still wore girdles and ratted their hair into nests and bee-hives?

"In the corner, please, quickly, quickly." Sarah clapped her hands and the herd of females began moving across the floor. "Neat lines of two please. One *and* two *and* –"

Robin hated this part. She could never get the timing, she was always up when they were supposed to be down. Besides, all the hopping and jumping made her lose control of her bladder, a spinoff of childbirth. Once a year her gynecologist tried to convince her that it would take only minor surgery to correct. But Robin couldn't be bothered.

"Faster, faster," Sarah called, as the rows of dancers moved across the floor, leaps and bounds combined with hops and dips. Reaching the far end, they quickly walked to the opposite corner for another round.

Three times across the dance floor and Robin was panting with exhaustion, her heart pounding. She had loved Peru, and she had almost loved her gentle colleague. But the bond had not been strong enough to cancel Central Park or the North Sea. They knew it was over when they traveled to Machu-Picchu together, eager to convince themselves of their union. When she finally saw it – the place that had drawn her as a child flipping through *National Geographic* – it was quite clear that her life had been an error, a quirk of nature and time. She no more belonged to Central Park and the 20th Century than she belonged with the Dutch ethnologist. Machu-Picchu was where she should have been, on that piece of earth, under that sky, climbing those steps, cut from that mountain.

Robin watched as Sarah finally smiled and clapped brightly, thanking the class for a job well-done. She would see them all next week. Feeling fat, old and foolish, Robin walked towards the heaps of jeans and coats by the dance studio door. Where was her ability to soar? Where was her need to learn, where, her inclination for beauty and love? What would her mother have said? Thank God she wasn't alive to see her now, Robin mused, dropping to the floor to change her shoes.

"Our class was exhausting. How was yours?"

Robin looked up. Marla stood mopping her face with a towel. Margot was exercising her neck and shoulder muscles. They looked wonderful, and Robin wished they were both still young enough so she could kiss them in public, then and there.

"Alright. Can I buy you girls lunch?" She asked, tying up her shoes.

The girls looked at each other. "Actually Mom, we were going to meet some of the kids – " Margot looked apologetic.

"That's fine, I just didn't want you to go without eating."

"We'll be home by three," the girls called, hurrying off.

Robin waved. She remained inertly on the floor, staring past the open doorway, past the last dancers straggling out. What, she wondered suddenly, what would she have been in her other life? Amongst the Paracas, perhaps she might have been trusted with the embroidering of a great mantle for a chief. Sitting in her niche of a dusty, ochre Peruvian landscape, chewing coca leaves to ward off the cold, she would labor for years on the same task. She would eagerly interpret and relentlessly record the Paracas Gods that her eyes and coca-leaf psyche understood – human headed serpents, cat-like creatures holding trophy heads, birds and whales – the spirits of nature. Would a feverish determination eventually take control of her senses, or could a calm prevail until the last creature showed its articulate, colored outline? Robin reached for her sweatshirt and pulled it over her head. In another existence, she might very well have permitted creativity to consume her – bits of colored threads perpetually clinging to her dark skirts – even if, now, she wondered on which starless night she and her husband had lost each other.

   Robin stood up and reached for her bag. She would walk home, it was a beautiful day. What about the car? Bernard or Margot would have to give her a lift down in the afternoon, so she could drive it back. They would probably be busy and the whole thing would become complicated and confused. It was worth it, Robin decided firmly. Perhaps later she could call Charles Humphrey about that teaching offer. But first, first she would have to tell Bernard that she was going to leave him.

SON

"Your son will be a functional literate," the learning specialist said, slowly articulating his words as though comprehension might be a problem.

Tasha tried to ignore the fact that 'functional literate' had primed her adrenaline and turned her hands clammy. She concentrated on the small office: the desk with the papers, the blank, beige walls, the window over-looking construction on a new wing. They were in a child development clinic in Bloomington, Indiana, the good midwest. Tasha turned back to the learning specialist. He'd barely said anything, but she already disliked him intensely, especially his articulation of 'functional literate'.

Her husband, Richard, did the same thing, Tasha realized. When speaking to people for whom English was a second language, or if habitual 'tuning out' was involved, he formed the words carefully in his mouth before issuing them like immaculate pearls. She had often felt it must seem condescending; she'd much prefer to see him get on with his sentence, even if it meant having to repeat the whole damn thing. At times, a wave of irritation would cross the listener's face, perhaps a flutter of the hand, or a shake of the head, 'yes, yes, go on'.

"Could you elaborate?"

Richard's voice was defiant, haughty. Tasha was grateful.

"Certainly," the specialist nodded. "Although your son David will probably never read a book like *War and Peace*, eventually he'll be able to read his way out of an elevator."

Tasha was beyond speaking; her heart raced wildly, her face burned, her hands shook.

"Sounds terrific – "

The specialist acknowledged Richard's sarcasm with a dry smile. He leaned forward across the desk, looking intently from Tasha to Richard. "I've found David to be severely dyslexic."

A sickly, beige silence mushroomed in the small office.

Without looking, Tasha knew that Richard's face had drained to gray granite. She stared hard at the learning specialist's glasses, at his sallow skin, the nervous, thin lips.

Tasha catapulted backwards two years, to the San Antonio parking lot, to the heat.

"What happens in 'real' school if you can't learn?"

She could feel the Texas sun mercilessly beating down on the asphalt where she stood watching David, as he squinted in the light. He had exited the Creative World Preschool clutching some drawings, a half-eaten cupcake in the other hand. He had asked as they approached the car, and at four and a half, still round-faced, still baby-chubby, he waited patiently for her answer. His question had jolted her out of her own preoccupation with Richard's position, the University. It had become quite obvious in the last week that they were not going to tenure their Blake scholar.

"What happens Mommy, what happens?"

She was back. The beige silence still hung in the clinic office. Tasha felt a sudden burst of frustrating guilt and tears. During those last few months in Texas, and in the two years since they'd been in Indiana, this child had been burdened, alone, with something no one was ready to confront. Not that they hadn't realized long ago something was amiss – his difficulty with the alphabet and remembering names, his 'chronological immaturity', as the school called it, the hyperactivity, the inability to sit still, and finally, his repetition of grade one – but both she and Richard hoped it was the famous developmental difference between boys and girls, or perhaps a question of priorities and maturity. Richard turned to her as she fumbled in her purse for a Kleenex.

"Are you all right?" The specialist focused on Tasha.

Tasha nodded silently.

"I've never had a parent react this way," the man said uncomfortably, perplexed. "Usually they're quite relieved to have a handle put on their child's problem." His voice softened, "I know how disappointing this diagnosis must be, but I assumed," he turned from Tasha to Richard, "I assumed you wanted to hear the truth."

"Of course," Richard acknowledged professionally.

Tasha cleared her throat. She didn't have to act professional, she was the child's mother, and this man was obviously part animal. "Are you always so confident, so cut and dry about your predictions and the future? Our son David is only seven." Tasha was blunt, her voice tight, unyielding. Of course it was an accident of fate. How was the poor man to know that at the age of sixteen Tasha had spent a summer with *War and Peace*, reading and mulling and loving every minute of it. How was he to know that it was because of that book that Tasha would submit to literature, permitting the likes of Tolstoy to stake a claim on her soul.

"No one can ever be certain." The man's voice was calm, controlled. "I'm using statistics based on years of research. The results of the small tests I conducted on your son show that his short term memory functioning is severely depressed. I believe the school psychologist had similar findings." He stopped and searched his desk top for a copy of the school report. "Here we are – problems with word retrieval, depressed functioning in memory for sentences, questionable visual retention – " He looked up from his reading. "Sight words, words that he cannot sound out phonetically, will always cause him some problems. Let me show you, it might be easier." He picked up another paper from his desk. "I asked him to spell the word eyes, e-y-e-s. Do you know how he spelled it?" He glanced from Tasha to Richard.

They looked blank.

"I-i-s. Not a bad guess really, nevertheless, a child of his age should be able to spell *eyes*."

"But from the word *eyes*, how do you get to elevators and *War and Peace*?" Tasha asked impatiently. She felt bruised and defensive. She had hoped, and she knew Richard had too, that perhaps David's reading progress had been hindered because of a pyschological barrier. After all, those first few months of grade one had caused him great anxiety.

"Statistics. Before I forget, sometime this afternoon I'd like to give you both some reading tests, if you don't mind, that is. Occasionally it helps us to pinpoint the child's problem," the specialist explained.

Reading tests? She could not have heard correctly, Tasha assured herself. A writer, and Richard a Blake scholar, and this person was proposing reading tests?

"Now, let's focus for a minute on what we're going to do about David. What I would like to see is a program whereby your son can learn through his ears, rather than his eyes, i.e., tapes, records, reading buddies. It will not be easy working it through the school system; they've always been adverse to alternate systems of learning. Believe me, I know how hard it is for parents who want a literate education for their child. But you will have to begin treating him as though he is an intelligent blind child. As a matter of fact, he qualifies for state assistance to the blind and handi. . ."

"Does this mean you would not encourage him to read?" Richard interrupted, aghast.

Tasha was back in Texas.

"Are you going to finish that cupcake before we get into the car?"

"Tell me Mommy, what happens?"

He stood beside the opened car refusing to get in until she answered his question.

"What do you mean David?"

"I told you. What happens in real school if you can't learn?"

"That's why we have teachers, to help us."

"What if you can't learn, like other children?"

Standing in the sun made Tasha irritable, and now she was bothered by David's question. It was a scorching afternoon, still and dry. She looked out at the arid landscape between the preschool and the sprawling University. Grass never grew around the craggy, Texas oaks. There were isolated wild shrubs and flowers, but it was mostly parched, cracked earth. Focusing on the contemporary buildings erected on a discontinued oil field, she had to keep reminding herself that it was a young, raw campus. No one held claim to it. The city had older, neater, more established colleges. The state acknowledged it was a weaker branch in its network of campuses. The faculty grumbled. After all was said and done, it was probably a good thing the English department did not want a tenured Blake scholar.

"What if the teacher can't help you learn?"

"If he were my son," the learning specialist said, leaning towards Richard, "I would read everything to him, never putting him under pressure to perform."

"But he can't go through life without reading," Richard announced.

"He may just have to, and we'd be foolish not to admit that as a possibility." The learning specialist said firmly, releasing some flakes of skin that had collected around his thumb nail.

"I have trouble with that idea," Tasha blurted, shaking her head.

The specialist waited.

"How can you raise a child not expecting him to read? Besides, it's not as if he just can't." She turned to Richard, he nodded in agreement. "Why just the other day – "

"Look, don't misunderstand me, he'll always be able to read a little, but he'll never be able to read well. As I said, I'm going on statistics, years of research."

"I want to tell you about the other day," Tasha said. "We were at the printers, and he asked me to read him a sign on the Xerox machine. I told him to try. 'Please close the lod,' he read, quickly correcting the last word when he realized it didn't make sense."

"Of course, of course." The man said, dismissing the incident, patiently closing his eyes. "Like anyone else, he'll have good moments along with the bad. But we have to realize and accept that it will mostly be down rather than up."

* * *

Tasha stood out in the fenced in play area for a few moments speaking with David's San Antonio preschool teacher, watching the children. Yes, they had been looking at a few letters of the alphabet, and yes, David did have trouble remembering them the next day.

"But the other children didn't?" Tasha asked.

"No."

"And David was aware of that?"

"I don't think so," the teacher said, bending over to wipe a child's nose. "You know how children are, usually they don't pay attention to the things that concern adults."

Mostly down, rather than up? Tasha could not believe the prediction. "But isn't it conceivable that eventually it might all click for him?" she asked. "When I was a kid, I was a terrible reader, for years. It wasn't until grade seven that I really got into it. I asked Dr. Clapp this morning if it wasn't possible that David might be the same."

"And I believe Dr. Clapp told you that since you were not diagnosed as dyslexic, we have to assume you weren't."

"But no one even used the word dyslexia in those days! Children were simply labeled as slow readers. What if we follow your advice, and don't encourage David to read. What if years from now it turns out he's quite capable, but he's lacking the skills?"

The phone rang on the desk. The learning specialist reached for it. He listened, nodding, and said he was almost done.

"I'm conducting my own research project for my Ph.D." he said, changing the subject, "and if you don't mind, I'd like to use your son as part of my project. It would entail having him come down here to the center once a week to – "

"We'll have to think about that," Richard said cooly.

"Please do. Now, I'd like to discuss with you what I propose recommending to the school. I would suggest an auditory program that – "

Tasha sat back. It had been a long, grueling day. They were at the Center by 8:00 and it was now 4:00.

"Are they going to test my dumbness again?" David had asked that morning as they'd walked from the car to the clinic.

"They already know you're not dumb David, they've got all the test results from the school. They want to figure out why a smart boy like you has trouble with reading."

"O.K., so they're going to test my dumbness about reading." David repeated, jumping off the low wall he'd been walking on in front of the clinic.

In the next six hours he was seen by a psychologist, a social worker, a speech and hearing specialist, a physician and last, this learning specialist. She and Richard had been seen by the social worker and the physician, Dr. Clapp, with whom they were to have a last session to go over the results of the staff meeting.

The learning specialist was still explaining about a suitable learning program.

"I'm sorry, but we don't have time to get to those tests this afternoon," he said, glancing at his watch. "Another day. He's a very likeable little boy, and I've enjoyed working with him." He stood up and reached across to shake hands with Tasha and Richard. "Please think about letting me include David as part of my research."

David was waiting for them in the lounge. He looked tired. Tasha could no longer recall which tester had suggested David to be a rather unfriendly, morose child, with an obvious hoarseness and tightness of voice due to apprehension about the testing. It was the same person to point out his lack of social sensitivity as shown by his interruption of the tester. Tasha smiled.

"Can we go home now?" he asked, kicking his feet against the chair rung.

"Soon," she said, winking at her son. She thought of how they'd stopped at the gas station early that morning before starting out for the clinic. A young man they'd never seen before was tending the gas pumps. He approached the car and bent down to the driver's window, asking Richard politely how he could help them that fine morning. He seemed unusually solicitous and eager. Tasha was taken aback by his politeness, but before she had time to formulate a statement, David, who had been leaning curiously over the front seat between his parents, suggested that the fellow must be new at the job, and furthermore he would not last long. He had been in his usual bright, morning mood, stating his words confidently as fact, rather than opinion.

But he could not spell e-y-e-s.

Seated behind his desk, Dr. Clapp cleared his throat and began speaking in a subdued, monotoned voice. "Although I'll be giving you a copy of our findings, incidentally, we also send one to the school and another copy to the family physician, I'd like to go over some of the main points with you." He looked down at the multi-paged document. "We've found David to be a healthy, normal youngster, with an above average intelligence – "

That evening, at bed time, Tasha sat on David's bed. She talked and talked, her voice reassuring and gentle. She told him about Woodrow Wilson, Nelson Rockefeller and all the others who saw their words scrambled and reversed, or as meaningless configurations. She told him of their determination and accomplishments. David looked small and doubtful as he listened silently, his hands clasped behind his head, the sheet pulled up around his waist.

"You don't believe me, do you?" Tasha said quietly. "You think I'm saying it just to make you feel better?"

David shrugged. "I don't know."

"David, do you remember a few months ago when you took apart that old radio, remember all the wires and tubes and coils?"

David nodded, his eyes concentrating with curiosity.

"Our brains are like radios, wired and complicated, but they're better, because no two brains are the same, no two people are the same. One person might tune into things others don't even know exist. Another might be able to make colors no one has seen, or perhaps hear like no one else. Some people can figure out new things, new ways. The trick is to learn how your brain is wired, so you can make it work for you. It's not supposed to work for anyone else." Tasha stopped talking. David nodded seriously, straining to keep awake.

Did he understand, she wondered, watching her son silently for several moments, as sleep hovered over him. He looked seven, with his sandy hair and freckles, the dirty fingernails and ball point doodles on the back of his hands. Tomorrow he would awaken to a new day, a new world to conquer. His lids were beginning to close. Tasha leaned over and kissed him on the forehead. He turned over on his side and snuggled under the blanket.

"Mom?"

"Yes?"

"Do you think I'll ever learn to read?"

"Of course, David, I'm sure of it."

LIVIA AND THE GYPSIES

The night the gypsies came to the Pension Tarragona, the children's mother, Mary Sobral, made it quite clear they were not to speak with them. While she put out the alert – old Mrs. Forsyth backing her up, blue English eyes sparkling, white head bobbing – Mary's glance lingered longer on Livia than the others. This situation was not a problem for the eldest, Daphne, a shy and serious young lady, always well behaved. As for the younger boys – so close in age they shared a world not unlike that of twins – they were too young and too busy to care. But for ten year old Livia, it was her moment of agony and ecstasy. She was a free-spirited, inquisitive child, so when the entourage descended on their distinctly hum-drum and monochromatic establishment, Livia was smitten.

The family was to spend Juan Sobral's sabbatical year in Spain, for the children, and for Juan. Despite his American citizenship and the fifteen years of teaching philosophy at Yale, Juan was, and always would be, a Spaniard. Rigid and quiet, deeply engrossed in his writing, he had traveled from New Haven to his beloved Madrid, a familiar environment, to quietly pursue his work. Mary, while nervous about gypsies, was exceedingly American and overwhelmingly enthusiastic. Having been a Spanish major in college, she hoped to instill her children with the romance and virtue of an Iberian experience. After all was said and done, they were a relatively bilingual household, so language was not a problem. Biding their time, waiting out the month of October so they could move into the apartment November 1st, the pension became a time of limbo.

Mrs. Forsyth, or Mrs. F., as the children affectionately called her, was the only other regular guest who spoke English. She had lived most of her married life in the Far East, the wife of an English diplomat. Spending several months in Spain with her son, Dr. P.D. Forsyth – a world authority on the Alhambra – Mrs. F. had elected to remain in Madrid while he traveled to Granada to test his most recent theory regarding the engineering of the Alhambra Lions. Favoring mauves and violets, Mrs. F. was a kindly, peculiar old lady, taken to lapses of memory, and strange, sudden utterances about people and places in her past. One evening, while dining alone at her table, an exciting realization struck – just after the soup, and right before the salad course.

"It's Moira's birthday in England!"

Her words burst through the quiet dining room. The other guests looked up momentarily, no semblance of empathy in their heavy eyes, before turning back to their soup plates.

Despite Mrs. F.'s tendency to natter on, the children had quickly gotten used to her. Being alone, and on rather shaky ground as far as the language was concerned, she attached herself to the Sobrals, much to Mary's insistence, and the children acted as her interpreter, much to Juan's bemusement.

The gypsies arrived late one evening about 10:00, just as the regular pension guests were politely yawning in the lounge, stirring and making signs that it was time for the world to retire. American children were destined for an odd existence in that Madrid pension. The Spanish custom of eating dinner around nine, and therefore not retiring until after ten, was cause for excitement. The late hours were not a problem for Daphne or Livia. But the boys generally fell asleep in the afternoon to tide them through the dinner hour. By evening they were full of energy, chasing and bouncing around the satiated, groggy guests like a "now you see them, now you don't" magician's trick. Although patient and enthusiastic, Mary got crashing evening headaches, and Juan escaped behind the Madrid newspaper.

When the gypsies pushed through the wooden lounge doors, the apparition was nearly blinding. With every step, there was jingling and clinking and rustling of colorful cloth. Flashing gold and sparkling stones, long, maroon fingernails. Red lips and deep, mellow voices, laughter. The blue-black of the women's long curls and the men's hair and mustaches, gleamed in the yellowish pension light. While most people would be exhausted or at least paled by such a journey – the children overheard them telling the pension owner, Doña Santiago, that they'd come up from Seville on the train – the gypsies were flushed and excited, as though the evening had only just begun. In no time they were petting Doña Santiago's little grandson, Antonito, cooing and calling him loving names. Livia was insanely jealous. When the largest gypsy woman leaned closer and asked him rather loudly whom he loved more, his mother or his father, Livia heard her mother hissing under her breath to her father 'I told you they were gypsies!'. With that, they were all whisked off to bed, despite Livia's pleas that they wanted to hear how Antonito would answer.

Much to Livia's disappointment, the gypsies were not at breakfast the next morning. She wanted to ask their whereabouts of the old waiter who looked after the tables, but her mother forbade her, saying it was none of her business, and besides, they were probably sleeping. If she hadn't been so frightened of Doña Santiago, Livia would have asked her. In reality, everyone was afraid of Doña Santiago: her son, her son's wife - whom they saw only at meal time as she scurried from the kitchen to the laundry – the servants, even the guests. Hardly a dinner went by that Mary didn't whisper something to her husband about Doña Santiago's despicable treatment of all concerned. Only her grandson Antonito could do no wrong.

Doña Santiago was a tall, imposing woman, large-framed, large-bosomed, and with a fine tooled beak for a nose. Livia lied when she told Daphne she wasn't scared. Doña Santiago had once announced to Livia, while watching her work in her journal at the lounge writing desk, that the good Virgin – she nodded towards the painting hanging above Livia's head – that the good Virgin would eat her eyes out if she persisted on writing with her left hand. When Livia reported this event to her parents, they suggested she do all her writing in the privacy of their rooms. Having been brought up totally ignorant of all religious institutions and beliefs – Livia's parents were of the 'less is better and none is best' school of religious thought – Livia was quite impressed with this Virgin's power, given her lovely and innocent face. No matter how many times and in how many places she saw her portrait, she always appeared as a wistful and pretty young woman, with dreamy eyes.

In the late mornings, while the chambermaids cleaned the rooms and the two girls in the kitchen began work on the main meal, the children were sent to play in the lounge so as not to get in the way. That morning Daphne had gone to the library with their father so Livia was left to her own devices.

After making sure her brothers were hard at play and that her mother was engrossed in her correspondence, Livia decided to explore the "off limits" corridor. She knew it led past more guest rooms, another bathroom, and ended in the Santiago's private rooms. Doña Santiago had asked that "the children" not play in the corridor, probably not wanting to hear noise. Knowing the gypsies had been accommodated in that direction – it was impossible not to hear the guitar music – Livia soon found they had been given several adjoining rooms, and to her great excitement, all the doors were wide open.

She walked past once, feigning disinterest. No one saw her. The second time she slowed up, glancing into the room the music was coming from. A large smiling man sat on the bed, a guitar in his arms. Livia hesitated at the door.

"Come in, come in, don't be frightened!" He waved his arm around the room generously. Two women sat at the dresser engrossed in conversation. The man's shirt was unbuttoned and he was smoking.

She had no time to think about what her mother would say.

"What is your name?" He played more quietly as he spoke.

"Livia," she said, creeping in, hands behind her back, fingers feeling the cool walls.

"I am Carlos!" He touched his hairy chest with his spread fingers.

"Where are you from, my dear? Livia is such a beautiful name!"

"Connecticut," she answered, glancing around quickly. The two women stopped talking and looked at her curiously. The room was in complete disarray; there were clothes and boxes lying about, boots and instruments piled on the bed.

"Estelle, look, the little girl is a Connecticut Yankee!"

A long neck and curious face appeared around the doorway of the adjoining room. Cat-like, Estelle took one step out; one leg, one half of her upper torso, one arm. Finally, the other half pulled out. She wore a silky, opened red gown over something short and flowered, over something long and black. Her dark hair cascaded down her bosom and back.

"Coon-neck-tee-cut." She pronounced it hesitantly. Suddenly scurrying to the far corner of the room – her hair and the colored silks flying about her like wings – she searched through a heap of belongings, and then returned with several books. Shyly, she handed them to Livia. *American English For The Foreign Born*, *Geography of North America*. "I learn," she said eagerly.

"Estelle, for the love of God, the child speaks Spanish!"

Estelle smiled but seemed disappointed not to have a chance to speak English. Languidly she walked over to the armchair and sat down.

Within minutes several other gypsies joined them. Livia was soon listening to their stories and music and telling them about her family. When she showed them the flamenco steps she had learned and told them she would love to wear a flamenco dress, Livia had the room in an uproar of laughter and clapping. They played and she danced and Estelle hurriedly searched through a bag for an appropriate dress. But seconds later, Doña Santiago stood in the doorway, frowning.

"I think perhaps you ought to return to your room, young lady. Your mother will be looking for you. And the rest of you, I've told you on previous trips that you cannot play those instruments in the pension. You are disturbing the other guests."

The room quieted to grumbling and the gypsies began to disperse back to their rooms. As Livia walked down the hall, she could hear Doña Santiago asking Carlos to show her the jewelry they'd brought along on this trip.

Livia knew that in the evenings they performed at a club. She saw them coming and going in their wonderful clothes and make-up, their instruments and smiles. Her mother and Mrs. F. spoke at great length about the lives performers led. Livia overheard Mrs. F. saying that her own father had been on the stage, and from what she knew of such people, they were really quite harmless, and that she, Mary, shouldn't worry. It was then that Livia realized her mother knew about her late morning whereabouts.

She visited the gypsies several more times, conversing with Estelle in English and helping her with her accent. Estelle found dresses for her to try on, tucking them in at the waist, pinning them up at the hem. She let out Livia's pale braids, sighing at the fine, blond undulations, and then pinned in flowers and ribbons. Twice Carlos laughingly asked her if she didn't want to go with them. He promised to marry her and take her to Seville where she could be a flamenco dancer.

When they left, five days after their arrival, the pension faded to black and white. Livia watched from the window with Doña Santiago, her mother and Mrs. F. as the gypsies hired cabs in front of the pension. The weather had turned cold; the women wore scarves and bulky sweaters over their dresses. Carlos was wearing a sheepskin vest, but his shirt was still unbuttoned. Estelle glanced up at the window and blew Livia a kiss goodbye. Carlos held up his guitar and shook it in the air, smiling.

When the cabs finally pulled away, Dona Santiago left the lounge and grumbled about how untrustworthy they were, but Livia's mother and Mrs. F. seemed wistful, almost young. Livia bravely showed them the locket Estelle had given her.

"I guess it was alright to speak with them after all," Mary Sobral gently conceded.

Mrs. F. nodded in agreement, peering out the window at the sky. "There's a storm over Lebanon," she said matter-of-factly, lost in thought.

Livia was thinking that they had only three more days at the pension, three more days until the first of the month and their apartment. She had thought it best not to tell her mother that Carlos said he would marry her, and take her to Seville.

FIVE WHITE SHIRTS

On a subway in Barcelona I once saw a neglected little man wearing a newspaper for a shirt. He had it tucked into his pants and jacket, a quivering hand held it in place. His cheeks were flushed and his eyes looked feverish and distracted. He clutched the stainless steel rod near the door, and his head flipped back and forth as the posters and gum machines sped past. Somehow he didn't look like a subway bum. My staring must have been obvious; I felt the woman next to me tap my arm.

She had known him for many years, she said. They had grown up together in the same neighborhood; she knew the path of his life. She asked me if I wanted to hear his story; a tragic tale of patience and love, deceit and revenge. I nodded, intrigued, and so she began.

Some years ago, when things were different, many people, no doubt, would have called Alfonso Segundo 'a nobody'; merely a middle-aged civil servant, a Catalan, who happened to be soft spoken and genteel, like his mother, Doña Isolda. He was the sort of person who is passed on the street without so much as a blink of the eye.

While physically small and unobtrusive, his posture and walk gave the impression of pride and self-importance. He was always impeccably dressed, his white shirt starched, his dark suit well fitting and smooth over his rounded torso. His shoes were never unpolished, and he rarely went anywhere without his umbrella. Alfonso took pride in being complete and presentable. He wore his possessions at all times, cuff links, tie clasp, watch, ring. Wherever Alfonso went, whether it was the corner cigar store, or Las Ramblas, he was always the same; neat and sealed, like a parcel, ready to be mailed.

If by chance one happened to be standing next to him on a crowded subway at the end of a long day, he would still look as fresh and neat as he had in the morning. Despite the perspiration glistening on his forehead, his tie would remain tight under his collar. The lavender scent, lingering on his shaven, rosy cheeks, would finally make even the most uncurious, uncaring turn and look into his face. The inexplicable sadness in Alfonso's large, deep set eyes, shy and tired under the arched brows, could tighten stomachs. He had the face of a child, forced by nature and circumstance to grow up.

Just when did Alfonso's story begin? It would be difficult to pick a time or an incident. Possibly that brisk, April day, about a month before his pending wedding, would be as good a beginning as any.

It was Sunday again and mass was over. Alfonso Segundo slowly walked his mother home, listening sympathetically to her distracted, nervous chatter.

"Doña Anna, at the age of fifty, has finally had a child, a miracle! Little Nieves, the silly child, has run off with the butcher's son, and Don Carlos T. had enough gall stones removed to pave a road – "

Alfonso gently squeezed his mother's arm. He saw her delicate, troubled face tighten for a moment, and then turn away. His poor mother. As the time was drawing nearer, it was becoming more, not less difficult for her to accept. Today the priest had stopped to congratulate her. Now it was official; everyone knew about his forthcoming wedding.

As they entered Calle del Pino, Alfonso looked up towards their apartment. He often fantasized that some Sunday, miraculously, their apartment would be found lowered from the fifth floor to the first. Of course it never was. It always remained high up above the merchant's shops and jewelry kiosks. Five flights of stairs were getting to be too much for an old woman and her marketing. Alfonso worried about his mother, especially now, for soon he would no longer be living with her. What could he do? For years she had refused to move, and now of course it was worse. She was stubborn and pouty;

she refused to believe it would truly come to pass. Besides, he well knew how good apartments were so difficult to find in Barcelona.

"Never!" Doña Isolda said to her son, shaking her head slowly as they climbed the flight of stairs. She would never leave.

She loved their apartment, it was home, and they had a balcony. It was a tiny oasis hanging above the noise of delivery trucks and shouting and horns and crying that seemed as constant on the street below, as the sun was constant above. It was on that red tile balcony, where Alfonso's birds sang out from cages and where ancient geraniums basked happily in the sun, it was there that Isolda dreamt, there that she watched the world. No, she would stay just where she was.

Alfonso shrugged his shoulders and gently kissed his mother's forehead. Silently he unlocked the apartment door.

It was always tidy and still inside, the only sound was the ticking of an heirloom clock. Doña Isolda rarely pulled the drapes on the balcony door, for she well knew how quickly the sun would fade the sofa and the carpet. Although she aired the apartment every day, the perpetual staleness of cooked cabbage seemed as inevitable and normal as the quiet. Alfonso helped his mother off with her coat, and then stood by patiently as she took the black tule off her head and tucked it neatly into her coat pocket. He hung up her coat. While she rearranged her hair in the vestibule mirror, Alfonso shifted his feet, cleared his throat and straightened his tie.

She looked at him severely in the mirror. "You're going out again, aren't you?"

Alfonso nodded shyly. "But I'll be back in time to take you for our walk."

After Alfonso left, Isolda went to her kitchen and filled the sprinkling can with water. It was her custom to feed the birds and water the flowers on the balcony before the sun became too hot. It was also her custom to lean against the balcony railing and wait while her son climbed down the five flights of stairs.

When Alfonso stepped out onto the street, he looked up and waved to his mother. Isolda never failed to notice how tidy he always looked, but of course she took great care with his shirts. She watched Alfonso greet the neighbors. She watched him reach into his pocket and throw crumbs to the flocking pigeons. They seemed to know he would always remember to save a few crumbs from his breakfast roll.

It was a clean shirt every day. Every morning after Alfonso left for work, Isolda washed. In the afternoon, during the two hours when the stores were closed and it was quiet on the street below, she ironed the shirt, methodically. When it was pressed and stiff, she hung it over the back of a dining room chair.

He was a good son. On Sundays he took her out, anywhere she wanted to go. Naturally she was proud of him, despite – she shook her head. Isolda watched as her son disappeared at the end of the street, heading towards the subway entrance. She never took subways alone; she didn't have to. No, he was a good son. She refused to think about the other business; she refused to ruin her day.

Occasionally Doña Isolda was stopped on the street and asked about her son. Her eyes sparkled. Alfonso had inherited her dark eyes and arched brows. Her skin was so white and transparent, veins ran on her eyelids like roads on a map. When Isolda began on the subject of her son, she inevitably cocked her head to one side, abruptly disturbing her gold earrings, long and disdainful, like Victorian twin sisters. Isolda loved to talk about Alfonso, about his job at the large building on Colón Avenue, the building with the enormous columns and large letters at the top; TELEFONOS-TELEGRAMAS.

"Can you imagine, hundreds of people go into that building," she always added, with sheer amazement in her voice. As she spoke, the gold twisted and spun and danced, almost desperately, as if freed at last, yet protected by the folds of black tule hanging from her head. When she stopped talking, they too were stilled.

Isolda was leaning against the balcony, the watering can full. She sighed softly. Sometimes when she watered, she remembered the flowers that used to grow in her mother's garden in the village. She remembered other things, her childhood years at the convent, later her husband.

Shouting on the street caught Isolda's attention. She leaned over and looked down. Small boys in shorts were playing ball. Two older ones dressed in Sunday clothes were mounting bicycles. A young girl with an apron on was scurrying home with loaves of bread from the bakery. Women were coming out of their apartment houses, starting off for Sunday visits to relatives. Something Isolda saw caused a deep shadow to settle across her face; her poised watering can quivered, a taste of bitterness rushed through her mouth.

There were three things – besides his mother of course – three things that Alfonso loved, and he had loved them for as long as he could remember. One was birds, birds of any kind, even pigeons, the other was the Romanesque Museum on Montjuic, and the last was Margarita Carmel. How could he best describe his feelings for Margarita? It was difficult, and quite frankly, he was embarrassed and confused. They had been engaged for so many years, 21 to be exact, and he had wanted her so much for so long, that eventually something just seemed to burn out in him. It was different with his birds and frescos. A Sunday rarely went by that he didn't take his mother to Montjuic. He felt very happy there with the paintings and solitude. It wasn't like the crowds and noise of the phone office with its heat and stench, the telephone rendezvous with anxiety. The frescos were silent and at peace, their faces hard and judging, but lonely.

Years ago he had treated himself to a guidebook of the museum, and Sunday before they left on their walk, he carefully placed it in his jacket pocket. It was dog-eared and worn, and really he knew it by heart; nevertheless, he read and looked in silence. When he finished all the rooms, he would go back to the first one where his mother was waiting. She sat patiently under one of the enormous Christs. She never fidgeted or complained about waiting for him. Before they left, he would take her back to see something he found exceptionally beautiful that day. Dutifully she would look, her face and smile never betraying a hint of boredom. Then they would leave. Sometimes when the guards weren't around, Alfonso would reach up and feel the rough areas of color with his hand; he enjoyed leaving it there for a few seconds, flattened, limp. It was the coolness and serenity he wanted. Margarita was no longer cool nor serene, and she had never allowed him to flatten his hand against her, never, in all the years. Recently he had brought Margarita instead of his mother to Montjuic. Margarita, in turn, brought along her own mother. Old Doña Pilar annoyed Alfonso, she always had, but what could he say?

Margarita's high heels had clomped though the rooms while Doña Pilar, bewildered, shuffled along behind in black, felt slippers, one hand hanging onto her daughter's jacket as though it were a tail.

"So who have we here?" Margarita had asked loudly, swinging her purse playfully against a wooden statue while her mother tittered into the sleeve of her black sweater.

"The large Christ in the east room was discovered in the small town of Teruel —" Alfonso read, but Margarita and her mother stifled giggles as they pointed here and there, without looking, without listening. Finally, when utterly bored, the two women found a small window with a pathetic stream of light. Margarita stood there jabbing at her face with her lipsticks and powders, while her mother hovered nearby, keeping a sharp lookout for the guard. Alfonso had never felt quite so humiliated.

"Not until we're married," Margarita used to say, when Alfonso had wanted to touch her. Those walks and hot evenings seemed like years ago, and they were. Of course she wouldn't even consider marrying him and moving into his mother's apartment. No, there was to be no wedding until they had everything they needed for an apartment, their own.

"I'm only a civil servant," Alfonso used to complain. "It will take me a lifetime to save enough."

"No matter my love. The best things in life are worth waiting for," Margarita had said, smiling demurely.

So, for years Alfonso devoted Saturdays to Margarita, and Sundays to his mother. That April afternoon when he returned to his mother's apartment, he took her for a walk, as promised. Isolda felt like the Ramblas for her outing. Slowly, silently they walked, enjoying the flower stalls, the sun and the people. After an hour or so of walking, Alfonso always treated his mother to a coffee at one of the cafés. They sat for a long time sipping their drinks and watching people pass. Occasionally Doña Isolda would see something that reminded her of her past. Often it was a young man who resembled the blurry memory of Alfonso's father, shot during the Spanish Civil War. She was alone now, she had only Alfonso. His marriage was becoming a reality. Isolda knew he had nothing left to save for; she knew he had purchased everything Margarita had asked for. It had taken years, but he had done it. Was it really going to happen? Isolda still could not accept it.

That very morning on her balcony, with her watering can poised and that bitter taste in her mouth, Isolda had watched with horrible fascination as two large, slow moving women swayed down the street. Arm in arm, baskets in hand, they walked secretively, their heads put together. The older one, Doña Pilar, wore a dark kerchief pulled down low over her forehead; Isolda knew for a fact that she was almost completely bald on the top of her head. Strands of oily, straggly hair peeped out from under the kerchief around her neck. She wore a badly dyed black skirt and some kind of loose, black sweater. Her stockings too were black and very mended, and of course she wore her slippers, like so many women in the neighborhood. It was a habit Doña Isolda abhorred.

At first glance, the younger one looked respectable enough, with her dyed auburn hair and the white collar lying flat on the black suit jacket. But with a closer look, Isolda knew very well what she would find. The auburn hair was oily and black at the roots. Under her hair, the white collar had make-up and grease. The crevices of her face were filled with powder; the greedy lips reddened mercilessly. Her suit, black and exhausted with the memory of dead relatives, was tight across the belly, short in the sleeves. Isolda had heard it whispered on the block that when this woman found a grease spot on the front of her skirt, she merely turned it around to the back.

Isolda could well imagine the life these two women led. Early in the morning dawn, the older one scuffed around in the kitchen. Coughing and hacking, she rubbed her hands to ward off the chill as she fumbled in the dim light to ignite the kerosene burner for coffee. No doubt she slept with that dirty kerchief on her head. The younger one probably stood at the small dresser, yawning and stretching, as she sniffed, and finally powdered her blouse and armpits. Really, Isolda did not care to guess what went on underneath her suit, although she had a good inkling. Once in the market she had seen that unbelievably tattered slip unashamedly peeping out from underneath Margarita's skirt as she bent over a basket of oranges. Her skinny bare legs seemed glued into those felt slippers, and the slippers seemed quite at home absorbing the puddles around the fish vendor's stand. Saturdays of course were different. She left her neighborhood, so she wore shoes and nylons and carried a purse instead of basket. But Isolda seriously questioned whether she ever washed her fishy feet.

A shudder ran through Isolda; she shook her head. What could she do? Her son was a grown man; he was supposed to know what he wanted. But did he really want Margarita Carmel?

Alfonso was saying something. He had sensed that his mother was upset. Leaning across the small cafe table, his hand resting gently on his mother's, there was tenderness in his face as he spoke.

"Every Sunday Mother, I will come back every Sunday to take you for our walk." He straightened up. "Perhaps Margarita will join us," he added shyly, hopefully. But then he felt his mother's hand pull out from underneath his, withdrawing like a small, frightened rabbit.

She sat up straight, her face hurt and saddened.

Alfonso picked up his coffee again and turned away to watch people pass, to listen as they talked. Very young couples, arm in arm, whispered to each other, laughingly. The best things in life are worth waiting for, Alfonso thought, quite suddenly, for no reason at all. He blushed crimson at the thought of earlier and how he had thrown himself back on the bed at the new apartment. He had been alone, he had gone to have another look. He hadn't wanted to tell his mother where he was going, but when she looked at him in the mirror that morning after mass, he realized she knew. He had walked slowly through each room, and finally, the bedroom. First he smoothed the quilted satin spread with his hands and then he let himself fall back against the cushions. Sometimes he couldn't help wondering how it had all come to this. When they were out window shopping, and he had to listen to Margarita babble on about more furnishings, more drapes, more and more, it was hard to remember Margarita as a young girl. And yet, she had not been unlike these pretty young things passing him on the Ramblas with their bare arms and legs, their faces content merely with their small, happy secrets and the sunshine.

Alfonso put his cup down and turned his eyes away from the girls and their legs. It was almost an automatic response, still, and he was a grown man. He had never forgotten that cold, windy morning, years and years ago. He hadn't been more than twelve. It happened in the playground of his school, a boy's school, run by Jesuits. They were all out in shorts doing exercises, jumping to keep warm. Suddenly the priest made all the boys turn around and face the school building, their backs to the street. They had to wait like that for several minutes, only the priest's eyes strangely fixed beyond the schoolyard fence. When they were allowed to turn back, Alfonso saw a young girl with a kerchief on her head. She had long bare legs and was just reaching the corner of the street. She had been hurrying; something had made her walk quickly out of view of the school yard.

Alfonso had gone to a woman, from time to time, when he was younger. He had heard about her from the men at work. She lived in a room in the Barrio Gotico, high up in a crumbling building. She was ageless: the wrinkles, the dyed black hair, the rolls of white flesh. Alfonso had wanted her nameless as well. He had never been able to imagine her older. She lounged continuously in a stained, sand-colored satin dressing gown, but her face was meticulously made up. It was as though she was always waiting to step out, waiting to be asked, and she had only to throw on her dress. There were old, tasseled pillows on her bed, the kind that hang at the back of magazine and candy stands in train stations: Copenhagen, Hong Kong, Rio. Afterwards, flushed, Alfonso could think only of Margarita and his mother as he felt his way down the dark, cracking staircase. He despised stepping out onto the street and becoming one with the other waiting men. He hated their quick glances and smiles. They stood around, either waiting, or just curious. Some were toothless, their hands thrust deep into their pant pockets, their eyes watery and bloodshot. That too seemed like years ago. Was she still there, Alfonso wondered, the same room, the same pillows?

How had Margarita turned into such a large and ungainly, greedy woman? Now of course, was no time to question. He had finally finished paying for everything she had picked. The sofa, the bedroom suite, the stove, the refrigerator, it was all paid for. And now too they had finally gotten this apartment, and the wedding plans were set. Everything was new and shiny in the apartment. It felt very different from their place on Pino. He knew he could get used to it, after all, it really wouldn't be that different from living with his mother. He would come home every evening, and Margarita would have dinner ready for him, just as his mother did. They could have a good life together, even if Margarita was getting too old for a family.

Alfonso had gotten off the bed and walked out to the balcony; he looked down at the unfamiliar neighborhood. They were really fortunate to have gotten a place at all, even if it was on the outskirts of Barcelona. Their apartment house was one of many, all of them identical. They seemed like a series of enormous, standing cigar boxes. The whole area was nothing more than new concrete and excavation dirt. Untidy children ran around the unlandscaped grounds. Clothes already hung like rags from the occupied balconies. Margarita probably wouldn't allow him to bring his birds. He would miss them, but he knew his mother would take good care of them.

Doña Isolda's hand shook on the café table. She simply could not understand her son.

"Beautiful day, Doña Isolda," Margarita had shouted from the street that morning. She had smiled, looking up at the balcony, waving her basket at her future mother-in-law. Her red fingertips caught the sun like jewels. Margarita's mother, Doña Pilar, grinned, silent and toothless, nodding and holding her kerchief in place with one hand, as she strained her neck back to see up to the balcony.

Doña Isolda had nodded discreetly, holding up a tiny, quivering hand, the way a small, invalid queen might. She had to force herself to look at them, to be near them. Tears had shot to her eyes. What could she do? She watched as they disappeared down the street, the older one looking like a bag of potatoes on black legs, the younger one, Margarita, like some strange bird, its body far too heavy and off balance for its skinny legs.

She would never be a good wife for him; she wouldn't even know how to take care of him, Isolda thought, looking down at the café table and her coffee. After a few moments, a slow, strange look of satisfaction came over Isolda's face. When Alfonso asked her if she had finished her coffee and was ready to leave, Isolda smiled distantly and nodded.

At the end of the month, Alfonso and Margarita were married in the church where his mother attended mass. It was a small, relatively quiet ceremony, quiet with the exception of Doña Pilar's continuous sniffling. Later, the priest and the wedding party gathered in Isolda's little apartment for anise and almond cakes. Alfonso had arranged for train tickets to Alicante, where they would spend a five day honeymoon before coming back to their new apartment. Alfonso was very pleased that his mother seemed in such high spirits, wishing them well, and waving them off.

Alfonso Segundo took his five white shirts on his honeymoon, clean and pressed. The day before the wedding, Isolda had washed and ironed, quietly, like a cat with a secret. When she was through, five white shirts hung stiffly on the dining room chairs, polite guests bored at a dull dinner party. Alicante was the honeymoon site, but what happened there is another story. Nevertheless, they returned to the city on the evening of the fifth day, for Alfonso was due back to work on the following morning.

On the morning of the sixth day, Alfonso woke up in his new apartment. They had returned so late the night before, they hadn't bothered to unpack. After Alfonso washed his face, he opened his suitcase. For a moment he stared silently at the crumpled, dirty shirts. He glanced over to where he had undressed the night before; his suit was draped neatly over the chair, but as was his habit, he had crumpled up his dirty shirt. What was he to wear, he suddenly wondered? He turned to the woman, his wife, still lying in the shiny, veneer bed. She was on her back, her mouth hung open in sleep.

"What am I to wear?" He asked quietly, shyly. "I've no clean shirts."

The large, bag-like form in the bed grunted. Slowly, as if anticipating pain, it moved, inch by inch, until it finally flopped over on its belly like an enormous seal.

"Margarita, I've no clean shirts," Alfonso repeated, louder this time.

"Then wash one!" The rude voice rumbled forth, as if coming from a pit in the ground. She pulled the blanket up over her head.

After standing around his suitcase for several minutes, bewildered and self-conscious, wondering what to do, Alfonso finally picked up a crumpled shirt. Putting on that shirt was sheer agony; no pain had ever been greater. But he buttoned it up, silently, meticulously. Then he walked out to the balcony and looked down. It was all so unfamiliar, not at all like Pino. Tears, old and bitter tears, streamed down his face.

The woman next to me on the subway was silent. She shook her head.

"What happened then?" I asked, knowing the story was not finished.

"Eventually Margarita simply threw him out," the woman said quietly. "Her mother, Doña Pilar, moved in with her, and Alfonso went back to live at Pino."

"With his mother," I added.

"Oh no," the woman said, turning to look at me, surprised. "Didn't I tell you? Doña Isolda died shortly after Alfonso returned from his honeymoon. It's said on Pino that she died from guilt, for she had known full well that Alfonso would have no clean shirts when he returned to work."

Before I got off at my subway stop, I looked for him again, the little man with the feverish eyes and the paper shirt, but he must have gotten off long before.

FRIENDS OF THE TEATRO COLÓN

"And how do you find the Argentine, *un poco caída*, a bit fallen, yes?" The voice comes in small bursts, crackling sparkles sifting to the floor. Olga asks but answers herself, not having the heart to hear the awful truth from the mouth of an outsider. And yet, her small, intense eyes are hopeful, her mouth nervous. Olga is dark, with tiny limbs and a rather large head. Her proportions are nearly dwarf-like.

I, the outsider, visitor from the north, fumble for a discreet phrase, something polite about Argentina's wretched state of affairs in the months following the Falklands' War. I've come to Argentina in search of a past I never knew, a family I've never met. My aunt Eva, in turn, has brought me to the Colón theater, so that I might see what is still fine and grand in this country, so that I might meet her three dearest and oldest friends.

Olga drops her eyes to her coffee cup. To her right, the poet Magdalena sighs. To her left, the still beautiful Felicia shakes her head. Friends since infancy, they have remained inseparable. Together they have celebrated their milestones, together they have weathered their storms.

Endless rows of crystal and gilt chandeliers sparkle along the high ceiling of the Salón de Té. Waiters rush among the crowded tables. The noise level is high; talking, peals of laughter, even the occasional shout of recognition. Smoke drifts in the room as people light more cigarettes, shifting their chairs, engaging in new topics of conversation.

"Like Lautréc, is it not?"

I look across the table towards the voice. It is not Olga, but Magdalena, the poet.

"I'm sorry, I don't – "

"The scene, the whole Salón," she waves her arms. "I saw how you were observing. Does it not seem like Lautréc? The crowds, the elegant evening clothes, the smoking and drinking – you know his work?"

"Of course, you're quite right."

Magdalena nods approvingly, smoothing the white tablecloth with her dry palms. She wears no make-up. She lives simply, alone.

I have the feeling it's not the first time she's said this about Lautréc. I had been told about her disastrous marriage and the suicide attempt, the two slim volumes of poems and her yearly readings. Earlier, while my aunt Eva prepared dinner, she talked and talked about her three friends I would meet at the theater. She had spoken of their similarities and diversities, marriages and jobs, successes and failures. 'As for Magdalena's poetry,' her voice had quieted with hesitation, 'I think it's very controversial, but to tell you the truth, I don't keep up with those things.' Aunt Eva walked around the dinner table, offering flowered dishes as though they were after thoughts. 'Not that it matters you understand, because our closeness, our friendship, is uppermost for all of us.'

During my brief visit, I have come to love my aunt's poignant efforts at cheeriness, despite Buenos Aires' pervasive atmosphere of uncertainty and self-preserving denial. She's a steadfast optimist, a true romantic. I find myself flipping back ten, twenty, a hundred years, and then relocating her in an unknown, impressionist painting, something that might have been called "The Picnic." A plumpish young mother – abundant, reddish hair, beautiful skin – is caught in a moment of tranquility and observation. She watches as the sun's rays sift through the trees and dance on the white of her small children's stockings. If there are realities beyond the sun's rays, she is not destined to see them.

"A bit fallen, to be sure. Argentina, as you Americans say, is 'down in the heels.' Is this not how you say it?"

The third voice, Felicia's, soft and fluid, draws me back to the coffee table and the four friends, the Salón de Té.

I nod, smiling.

"But she will rise again, just you wait and see! Argentina will rise again!" Felicia, of the long suffering eyes and aristocratic bearing, elegantly dressed, raises her cup in mid-air, her hand quivering. Tragedy haunts this woman's life. Clearly God has put her on this earth to receive and store pain.

Olga, Magdalena and Eva join her, raising their cups, clinking, toasting their country like chimes on a summer night. Forty years of companionship, forty years of meeting twice a month at the Colón, attending opera, concerts and plays with their subscription tickets. There had been phone calls back and forth. A trip to the box office by Olga who worked close by, and finally, a shift in their seating arrangements. Olga went up to the next balcony, alone. All this, so that I might attend, so that I might sit next to my aunt Eva.

"Do we dare hope?" Eva pipes up brightly, her eyes twinkling, her cheeks flushed. She's excited, pleased I'm meeting her friends, pleased they're meeting me. For the moment, this engrosses her far more than Argentina's depressing circumstances.

"Yes – once again girls – Argentina will rise again!" Now it's Olga who leads the toast; but this time, somehow it sounds hollow, without vigor. The four sip their coffee silently.

"The theater is so beautiful," I offer. "And the music, it's breathtaking!" My aunt smiles approvingly.

"And the chorus, it must have close to a hundred voices." I continue.

"Exactly one hundred," Olga confirms.

"Would you like to stay for the second half? Mind you, it's long! We won't be out until after midnight." My aunt warns.

"Yes, please. I had no idea that I'd want to stay, quite the contrary, I – "

"Of course she wants to stay! How often do you get to hear St. Matthew's Passion in the Colón?" Despite what must be an unbearable burden of grief, Felicia manages a smile. "Right?" She looks me in the eye.

"Absolutely," I assure her.

"So, after all we too have *hermosura*, beautiful things?" Her voice is confident, almost reprimanding. She finally relinquishes her hold on an obedient, silk scarf and waves the air around her, indicating the Salón de Té, the marble halls and the theater beyond. I find her difficult, unyielding, hard.

"Argentina does have beautiful things," she repeats.

"Certainly," I smile. I have to give them that.

For indeed, Buenos Aires has the Colón. Its splendor and pomp and glitter eases the pain. It's one of the few public places not affected by the last forty years, its stateliness little changed since its first opera in 1908. The people still flock to it, eager to escape the reality of their time. The continual economic inflation and political subversion do not enter its doors. Felicia rides into the Colón on the waves of her time; elegant clothes and silk scarves, impeccable make-up on a face aged by anguish.

Sometimes he wails, for no apparent reason. The nurse on duty rushes to his side, but she can find nothing physical to cause the pain. The straps of his bib are not too tight, he has not soiled himself, nor has he dropped his crayons. A simple, plaintive wail, and for eight years Felicia has learned to accept it as his mode of communication. It has been eight years of caring for and listening to his miserably desperate soul, trapped in a healthy body, with a brain that has turned to mush. Total mush, all on a Sunday afternoon. It had been a bright sunny day that he had gone out to play the usual round of cards with his friends at the café. On his way home, he had paused long enough to drop all his money down a street drain – for no apparent reason. Shortly after that, his friends started complaining that there must be something wrong with Don Carlos, because he was cheating at cards, and he had never cheated before. That was only the beginning. The doctors called it premature senility. Felicia called it hell. One morning, shortly after he became ill, the doctor came to visit. He told Don Carlos he would have Felicia, his wife, get him some medication that would help him sleep. Don Carlos looked up at Felicia and winced.

"That woman is not my wife. I would never have married such a miserable soul."

Felicia wept, and then dried her tears. Although not her first, he had certainly been her finest lover, and he had always made her completely happy.

In the years that followed, Felicia took pride in the fact that she was able to keep him comfortable. He spent his mornings on the great, sunny, patio-porch, with the sliding glass doors that open out onto a garden of large leafed, tropical plants, palms and eucalyptuses. The gardener kept a bird cage in the far back, and for some time he'd been in the habit of bringing his two pet parakeets up to the porch on his arm. The birds sang out to Don Carlos, asking him repeatedly if he was better. But not long ago, one of the birds learned to imitate his wail. Naturally it was shriller than Don Carlos', but nevertheless, disturbingly accurate. Felicia had the birds destroyed.

Every morning they set Don Carlos out with his coloring in front of the television. They keep it on for him constantly. The incessant garbage of noise drowns out his small, animal-like sounds. Only the wails can be heard echoing through the long, old corridors. Felicia is glad now that she has decided to keep the house. She had considered selling it when her husband became ill, toyed with the idea of an apartment. But how confining that would have been for him. At least in the house he can be comfortable and private. He is exposed to no one, and no one is exposed to him. Their son, the architect, now lives in Rio. He comes to see his father twice a year, no longer bringing his wife and children with him. It is of course, too depressing for them. So Felicia is not only deprived of a husband, but of grandchildren as well. She does not travel to Rio to visit, for she would never leave him, whether he knows it or not.

Every night before she goes to bed, she thanks God that there is enough money to hire the staff necessary for his well being.

"To tell you the truth, Argentina *está muy baja*, very low right now." Another burst of words. Olga looks up at me. "It would be ridiculous to deny it," she adds.

I nod, understandingly, but I sense it is not my place to ask political questions. I watch as Olga begins to stack the cups and saucers, obviously driven to keep busy, either for the waiter's sake, or her own. The others watch her.

An active socialist all her life, Olga is the voice of the people. As a student she had joined the young university socialists, and within a few years, she rose to the rank of leadership. Although somewhat unattractive, she was an intelligent, committed girl, and she had the good fortune of being kind and unselfish. She fell desperately in love with another young socialist, who later went on to become a national socialist candidate. All her life she held secretarial or office-type jobs, just enough to maintain her, but nothing so demanding that it would involve her emotionally or intellectually. She held out for the party. As the years went on, her lover submitted to family pressures and married a wealthy girl, a union arranged by the two families. The marriage proved to be disastrous. Olga never married. She continued to live for the party and her lover. Both relationships were steadily maintained throughout the years. And yet, never once did she utter his name to her friends. It was for the good of his political career. But in her heart, Olga knew it would not have mattered. The other girls were not political animals; they did not care about all the factions of all the parties. They would not have searched the newspapers for his name; nor would they have followed his career, nor would they have told the butcher and the grocer that they knew his mistress. But Olga needed her privacy, and she respected theirs, and for this reason, she hardly ever spoke politics with her Colón friends.

"I don't believe our country has ever been so low." Olga says, staring sadly at the pile of cups and saucers.

"*Pero como*, Olga, how can you say that? What about a few years ago, when the military took over from Isabel Perón. What about the terror and disappearances, have you forgotten already?" Magdalena asks indignantly. "You know I lost a nephew," she lowers her voice, "you know my sister still marches in the plaza."

My aunt reaches over to pat Magdalena's arm. Concern shows on Felicia's forehead.

"Magdalena, none of us ever forgets those years," Felicia offers gently.

"Such depressing talk!" My aunt Eva straightens up. "We should all be ashamed of ourselves. This poor niece of mine will go back with a black view of Argentina!"

"Magdalena is right. The people suffered quietly, now they suffer out loud," Olga states.

They all nod seriously.

"She was once a great and fine nation." Olga looks at me. "In your schools, *amor*, do they teach the children about the history of Argentina? About Sarmiento, and all of his reforms?" She looks hopeful.

"To tell you the truth – " I begin.

"From what I understand, they don't even teach the children the history of their own country. How are they going to teach them the history of ours!" Magdalena states bitterly.

The lights begin to flicker on and off in the Salón. Women pull out their cosmetic bags and quickly dab and brush at their faces. Men put out their cigars. Intermission is over.

"Shall we?" Felicia asks, already standing.

We walk slowly through the Salón, the crowd pushing and swaying around us. It is several flights of stairs up to the third balcony, and my aunt clings to my arm as we climb the marble staircase.

"I hope you weren't upset by what Magdalena said about your schools." Her voice is low, almost a whisper. She knows Magdalena and Felicia are close behind us. "Sometimes she tends to be a little harsh."

"Not at all," I assure her.

"She really has had a miserable life, poor girl. Here we are!" My aunt steps forward and leads me into our aisle. We ease our way slowly, inching towards our seats.

"Don't you love the crowds?" My aunt asks cheerfully. "It's wonderful seeing people appreciate music, appreciate the Colón!" She speaks lightly, gayly.

"I've always wondered how those ladies with their big skirts ever managed to sit in these chairs. They're the same ones you know, the very same." She smiles, lowering her plump body into a tight, hard velvet seat.

"Look, 1909," Eva says, pointing up at the ceiling, and the date painted in at the foot of the fresco. Can you imagine the clothing of that time? Those enormous silk and velvet skirts, what a bother they must have been!" Eva adjusts herself in the seat and picks up her program. "The soprano is wonderful! I must say, though, I don't care at all for the tenor." She puts on her glasses and begins reading the program.

I watch as people enter and sit in their seats, adjusting, preparing, readying themselves. A comforting, quiet hum rises from the audience. An older couple enter our aisle and begin working down towards their places. All those sitting have to stand to let them pass.

"You know," Eva says, easing herself up, "It's really a shame you can't stay in Buenos Aires just another few days."

"What will I be missing?"

The couple passes, Eva lowers herself again.

"Magdalena will be reading her poetry."

Once a year Magdalena was invited to read her poetry at the Society of Women Poets. She read at the San Martin Cultural Center. Chairs were set up in the lobby-like space, and Magdalena, in flowing charcoal chiffon, sat with the other poets. When it was her turn, she rose and moved to the podium like a ghost. Her voice was shrill, but she read with passion and conviction. She wrote about love.

The Colón friends always went, naturally. They arrived together, sat together, and left together. They never discussed Magdalena's poetry, nor did she with them, anymore than Olga talked politics. Merely their love and support for one another was enough. When my aunt Eva was periodically hospitalized for weeks on end with her back problem, they all came faithfully to visit, as often as they could. Two years ago, when Magdalena finally decided to leave her husband after twenty years of marriage, they all supported her completely. Of course, with her suicide attempt just weeks before her decision, what else could they do but support her?

Emilio Esquilache was a tall, dry man who spent most of his waking hours totally engrossed in his legal practice, and in the management of his inherited acres of ranch land. He was far too busy for children, or for that matter, for love and poetry. He awoke, ate breakfast and left for work at precisely the same time every morning. The only occasion their paths were sure to cross, was at breakfast, when Magdalena sat opposite him at the long table. She daydreamed as she stared at Emilio's rings and watch and cuff links. His nails were always immaculate, his collar stiff, his hair perfect. The silver gleamed, the napkins, snowy white. She had never seen him shave; she had never seen a tarnished knife nor a stained napkin. That was the problem. She had never felt in control of her life in this house. It had never been her house, but rather his family's. Not that his mother lived with them anymore. She had been in a home now for several years, but somehow she was still present. Whenever Magdalena gave the servants orders, they frowned and mumbled something about how Doña Clara would not do it that way. For God's sake, Magdalena thought, as Emilio tapped at his soft boiled egg, it had been twenty years, and still, nothing in the damn house was of her doing or choice. It always amazed her how Emilio could remove the egg's cap so neatly, precisely. The pantry door swung open, the flash of gleaming white tiles on the wall, and the cook entered the dining room with Emilio's coffee. She placed it gingerly in front of him. He nodded, without looking up from his paper.

"Café, Señora?" The cook asked.

"Yes, please." Magdalena watched her disappear again through the swinging door. Every morning she played a game to see how many tiles she could count before the door closed.

"Have you plans for the day?" Emilio asked, not bothering to glance at her.

"I haven't thought about it yet."

"I do wish you could find something to do with yourself Magdalena." Emilio wiped his mouth and stood up, glancing at his watch.

"Yes."

"I will have clients until late tonight. Do not wait to dine."

A perfunctory kiss, and he was off, the scent of Spanish lavender trailing behind.

She had plans, but in the end, they didn't work. She didn't take enough pills, and the maid found her semi-conscious at four in the afternoon.

"Did you enjoy it, my dear?"

My aunt Eva, her cheeks flushed and eyes red around the rims, wrestles with her short fur jacket that has slipped down behind her back. I reach over to help.

"Very much so."

"Good. Now let's see how quickly we can get out and find cabs."

It's a long, slow descent. People are tired and crowding, eager to be home. The marble floors and stairs seem harder than they did before. I can no longer see Magdalena and Felicia ahead of us in the crowd. I feel the weight of my aunt's weariness, as she leans towards me for support. Her back must be hurting, I realize. It was probably too long a time to be sitting. Finally, the huge, impressive doors, and cold air.

Magdalena, Felicia and Olga are waiting for us, huddled together under one of the street lights in front of the theater.

"*Otra noche en el Colón!*" My aunt says, approaching her friends. She turns to me, about to explain.

I nod, understanding.

They shiver and yawn and embrace good-bye. Magdalena and Felicia leave together in one taxi, both living in the same district, and Olga alone in another.

My aunt hails a cab. As we climb into the back seat, I ask if they've really been attending performances for the last forty years.

"Since we were sixteen!" She smiles and leans forward to give the driver directions.

"And during all those years – the Perón era, and when he returned with Isabel, the military governments – didn't you talk about what was going on?"

Aunt Eva reaches up and gently taps a finger to my mouth, making the same hushing sound one utters to a restless infant, unable to sleep. "We tried not to."

I ask no more.

As the taxi pulls off, she snuggles up against me, sighing happily.

NO PEACE AT VERSAILLES

—Train from Versailles to Paris—
4:10 p.m., August 15, 1986

I'm not a writer. As a matter of fact, I've never done anything like this. The idea of Paul Rubin keeping a journal seems ludicrous. I'm an economist, I teach at the University of Chicago, I make my living as a consultant. Naturally I've written scholarly articles, but I've never recorded anything about myself, what I see and do, what I think, feel. I really don't know what possessed me, the idea of a journal. A few days ago, on the way back to Paris from Giverny, the middle-aged English lady in our compartment was scribbling in a tiny, mauve notebook. Giving in to my curiosity, wondering if she had unearthed Monet's secret to color or light, I finally leaned close enough to see. She was simply listing the flowers – day lilies, anemones, irises, geraniums – she would pause, glance out the window for a few seconds, then smile and jot down some more. I have no desire to list flowers, so maybe the idea came because we told the kids they had to keep a journal of the trip. Or perhaps I'm compelled to record because I know that Emma is losing her hold again, and while away, I have no one to turn to. Since our arrival in Paris she's become increasingly nervous and preoccupied. At times she hides it very well, and then the smallest thing can set her back into a state of anxiety. She falters and slips, and before I can help, she's calling to me from those awful depths. The children, Penelope and Tony, have fallen asleep on the seat facing ours; they lean against each other like rag dolls, Penelope's dress crumpled, traces of chocolate yogurt around Tony's mouth. Emma is beside me, her breathing heavy in sleep. The rash has completely disappeared, her neck and face have cooled to ivory, hints of the sun on her cheekbones and nose. Even in sleep she looks anxious and fragmented. Don't let her fool you. She's a master of deception, believe me. The logical place to begin today's entry is the beginning, at breakfast. But knowing Emma, I doubt that's how she would do it.

The line of people extended all the way down through the Ministers' Court and out the gilded gates. Emma realized she was already impatient and hot. The sun was very strong. The woman in front of her, wearing a Coca-Cola T-shirt and speaking English, explained that it was Monday, and the museums were closed in Paris. The man in front of the woman turned around to disagree; it had nothing to do with the museums in Paris, Versailles was always crowded. That's what his sister-in-law had told him, and she was Parisian.

It hardly mattered, Emma thought irritably, glancing at her arms, nervously feeling her throat. A few minutes ago, while reaching out to help her son Tony adjust the camera around his neck, she'd been confronted by the familiar, red rash starting up her arms, a mass of angry, raised skin. Now what had triggered it? Paul insisted she was overly preoccupied, that she brought it on just by worrying. The doctors said it was tension, there was nothing wrong with her skin. Jerks, all of them. So what then? Was she losing her mind? For the last two years was she simply imagining this horrible thing on her arms and neck, and the itch, the itch that would drive her crazy for several hours before subsiding. Extreme temperatures and over exposure to the sun didn't help matters. She knew that much, and she knew relief, relief that could only come from a cooling shower. One of these days, while waiting in line for some museum or palace to open, or pushing along a crowded street, or simply sitting in a warm park, one of these days, she would kill for a shower. She'd been keeping track, and in the last couple of months it had happened at least once a week.

'It's not normal,' her mother's voice had rung out over the phone just before they'd left for Paris. 'It's not normal at all, and if the doctors still haven't figured it out, they can't be up to much. Really dear, I don't see how it can be good for you, constantly breaking out. Problems with Paul again?' Her mother was a jerk too. 'Why won't you come to Connecticut, we'll get you appointments. If that doesn't work dear, Daddy and I will take you wherever it's necessary. Do you understand, Em? Wherever, just the three of us.' It was typical of her mother to ignore facts and reality – there was nothing slovenly about the University of Chicago medical school – but then her mother would find a euphemism for life, if she could.

"Hard to know how long it'll be before we get in," the man said, the one whose sister-in-law knew everything, because she was Parisian.

Emma shrugged, not wanting to converse with him. They were here, stuck approximately halfway along the waiting line. Emma knew she would have a rough, miserable afternoon. Would they wait it out? Surely it wasn't a wise decision. She hated crowds, and now with her skin – of course she knew enough not to touch or scratch, but she still wouldn't enjoy anything – and Paul hadn't wanted to come in the first place. He could be so trying. At breakfast, while she had been reading to the children from the guidebook, he kept interrupting, nonchalantly telling them how he despised excess and decadence, how if he visited Versailles one more time – he said that because her mother had been seven times, and the children knew it – one more time, he might become a communist, or at the very least, a socialist. The thought of all the gilt and brocade and marble made him want to vomit.

"Communist?" Tony had repeated, wide-eyed, his napkined chest pressed against the round café table, his little mouth about to be jammed with croissant.

"Socialist isn't as bad," Penelope had announced cooly, reaching across her younger brother for the jam. Emma knew their twelve-year old daughter was feeling rather grown up with her numerous plastic bangles and her fresh little sun dress. During their two week stay in Paris, she hadn't worn the dress once, intentionally saving it for Versailles. It would be an understatement to say that Penelope had a fixation about Versailles. Ever since her maternal grandmother's last French tour, when she'd brought back that Versailles parapher-nalia for Penny, the child was off and running. She had read the guidebook section on Versailles four times, and she was determined to see the queen's chamber and the Hall of Mirrors, much to her father's dismay.

"Daddy's just irritable this morning," Emma had said, picking up her coffee.

> In the past, one of the first signs has been that she accuses me of being irritable or anti-social when we disagree. Yet at breakfast, while she was reading to the children about Versailles, certainly not one of my favorite places, she seemed to be fine, at first anyway. As a matter of fact, she looked wonderful in her sexy French T-shirt and blue jeans. Sipping from the steaming cup, her curly red hair still damp from the shower, she looked more like the kids' baby sitter than their mother. Her long, fine fingers held the guidebook, extra napkins and her coffee. She kept reading and reading, her bag and the large, straw hat on the chair beside her. There's a natural leisureness about Emma, as though she spends great portions of everyday at café tables, patiently reading to, or tending children. Squinting in the sun, occasionally puffing on a cigarette, she enjoys watching the passing crowds, but always with the safety of distance, and with a shade of bitterness in her eyes. Does she see herself as out-of-step, unable to join in? Her motions are so well timed, so graceful, she can reach over with fresh napkins for Tony, or wipe up a spill of hot cocoa without interrupting her reading. You're probably wondering how I could even think there's anything wrong. It confuses me too; periodically I feel I'm the one who's unstable. But then something timely happens, and I know I'm right. Like this morning. At one point while she was reading, I buttered another large slice of bread and spread it with brie. After a few moments I realized she had suddenly put her book down and was watching me, her eyes inexplicably hot, angry. I must have wiped my hands on my jeans. It makes Emma crazy when I do that. It bothers her mother too. The woman is always making comments about my wearing sandals without socks, that kind of thing. I associate jeans with eating outdoors, and eating outdoors with never having enough napkins. In any case, Emma finally got back to her reading, but she was angry for the rest of the morning. She wouldn't even sit with me on the train coming out to Versailles. When she's like this, she tends to lose control – fatigue and melancholia, tears – then at other times, she's so together, mind and body, it's unbelievable. She has this knack, this remarkable knack of undermining me in front of the children – 'Daddy's just irritable this morning' – ever so gently, as if she isn't doing it at all. I hate it when she calls me 'Daddy' to the children. Her own father is still

'Daddy', Daddy this and Daddy that, Daddy said and Daddy did. For the most part, she does well ignoring her old, Connecticut family, established and bigoted. Home is a vine covered Tudor number, so dark and gloomy because of the 'marvellous stately trees', that the lights – stupid little shaded lamps everywhere you turn – have to be on during daylight hours. The place smells staid and stale, like predictable, boring upholstery and unseasoned, boiling beef. But occasionally, when she wants to rile me, she permits her ancestry to seep through to her long, lithesome exterior, wearing it, flaunting it. At such times, it becomes her a little too convincingly. Odd that she should have spoken of Yves Maldeau this afternoon. It's been years since his name has come up in conversation. Am I still bothered that he was first, Emma's suitor and lover, while I, merely friend? Am I still nervous that he wanted me too? Perhaps, but I'm not about to pursue it. There are other things more pressing. I do wonder how much the children understand. Do they understand something is amiss? She loves them, I know that, she would never abandon them. Do they understand?

"Have you told them about Marie Antoinette and how she got her head chopped off?"

"Honestly, Paul, why do you have to be so gruesome?" He was getting back at her, Emma knew that. She had told the children he was irritable, and now he was getting back at her.

They all heard Tony swallow his milk.

"Mary who?" he asked.

"Marie, not Mary! Marie Antoinette. Oh my God, I am *so* embarrassed!" Penelope hissed under her breath towards her brother.

Finally, after breakfast, Paul had come along. Emma told him he could use the time to do something else, that she really didn't mind taking them alone to Versailles, but he came, grumbling all the way from the Gare du Nord to Châtelet.

They had been far too leisurely at breakfast. She hadn't thought, but they should have left early, and been here by 8:30 so they could be first in line. It was stupid to have to wait in this heat. The sun glistened on the palace's gilded balconies, on the tourists' glasses, on their cameras. Paul had gone off with the children to see if they couldn't get in some other entrance. It was then that she'd reached over to help Tony adjust the camera, and realized the rash was back.

Emma glanced at her arms. She knew her thoughts dispersed as quickly as they appeared – breakfast, her mother, the Coca-Cola T-shirt in front of her – this condition always made her go desperately blank, unable to focus and stick to one train of thought. Here she was, standing in line at Versailles, and she couldn't enjoy anything. She actually had to say to herself, now what am I going to think about? I should think about this, or that, or perhaps – It was so like Paul, refusing to believe he had to stand in line like everyone else, certain he could find another way in. She had always loved that about him, his aggressiveness, his self-confidence. They had left her with the lunch bag, and the shoulder pouch with the tickets and passports. She kept the lunch on the pavement, nudging it ahead with her foot as the line advanced. She had forgotten that even the cobblestones were excessive at Versailles; large, smooth boulders, rounded at the corners, like rolls beginning to rise.

"My father is an economic consultant."

Emma had heard Penny tell the American couple on the train ride out to Versailles.

"And my mother got her degree in history, but she hasn't done anything with it."

When Penny and Tony had heard English spoken two seats behind them, they had hurried back to sit with the American couple. Emma had given up trying to keep the children beside her on métros. Tony's lively blue eyes and curly, blond hair were his passport to the laps of smiling young Algerians and laughing, black students. Naturally she kept a hawk's eye on him, but he was in a perpetual state of happiness, despite the fact that a common language was nowhere to be heard.

As the RER C-5 line rushed through the suburban Parisian landscape, Emma could hear Penny deeply involved with the Americans, school, friends, who was taking care of their dog, and only occasionally did she permit Tony to contribute to the conversation. While Emma watched the passing, tiled houses and trained, candelabra-shaped pear trees in tiny, neat gardens, it was then that scattered memories of Yves Maldeau began floating back. The white shirt and pants, the laugh, the hedonism. He had not loved her half as much as she loved him. He was destined to go far with his brilliance and charm, his pushy New York mother and scholarly French father. He topped his class of Art History at Yale. He learned Chinese. His mother wanted him to have a diplomatic career. But there was a frailty and vulnerability, and besides, he wanted to write the definitive book on Ingres. They were so close that summer, the three of them always together, Paris, Provence, seeing and talking, the picnics.

Paul had taken a seat on the other side so he could face in the right direction. She knew it made him nauseated to sit backwards on a train. All the seats on his side were taken, or she'd go over and sit beside him, talk with him. She didn't think she wanted to be mad at him, all that stuff at breakfast about being a communist, or the silly thing of seeing him wipe his hands on his jeans. It frightened her the way she could be fine, feeling just fine, and then she could lose it, so suddenly, the smallest thing making her hysterically angry. They hadn't talked, really talked, since they'd been on this trip. They were slipping away from each other. Sometimes she didn't care, sometimes she wished she'd never married him. She hated it when she thought like that. She needed Paul.

He was reading, no doubt that economics text he'd brought with him from Chicago. How could he read an economics book in the middle of France?

Their marriage was suffering withdrawal and erosion. It probably had been for years, but she didn't know – they never talked about it. They only talked about the children. Was he going to pull out his book and read at Versailles? Was he going to be a pain in the ass there, talking about all the disgusting decadence?

Sometimes, still, when she looked at him, a tight excitement would form in the pit of her stomach. She remembered how he took her away from Yves, that morning, in the café. She was pleased, then embarrassed and angry that he could still excite her, still, even though she feared he was going to leave her.

> On the way out to Versailles, I know she was wondering how the hell I could concentrate on my book. I wasn't. I saw her watching me, seriously. I know she thinks I'm unrefined urban and aggressive, un-

trained for the more leisurely things, like gardens with gnarled wisteria, the light of Provence, art history. She's probably right. I like Paris, but it's different for Emma, at least it always has been. The museums and the parks, the French, the countryside, she adores it all, takes it to her heart and soul, it's as simple as that. I had hoped this trip would help re-channel the nervousness and anxiety. But when she gets strange, she pushes me away, she won't let me near. I love her, and I want her better, but what am I supposed to do? Our marriage has been an uphill battle, and I'm tired too. Her parents haven't helped, they've resented and disliked me from the beginning. God they've been awful. Maybe Emma should have listened when her mother tried to tell her our backgrounds were too diverse, the corporate lawyer father and the gentility of suburban New Haven, versus the Ma and Pa jewelry store and the streets of Chicago. They've put tremendous pressure on Emma. She loves them and wants to please, but never can, and she's always frustrated. If I had to give a time, a day when Emma spun off, and never really found her way back, it would be two years ago, with the stillborn baby. I don't believe she even realizes that's when it all began, the agitation, those strange inexplicable attacks on her arms and neck, the gaps, when her mind simply cannot function. I still hate myself for having allowed them to show her the body. But after the initial shock – when she was told the baby was dead – Emma became terrifyingly calm and together, demanding of us all, haughtily, that it was her right to see her baby. They finally acquiesced. It was horrible. The baby was grotesquely deformed, with hair growing all over. Afterwards she threw up and wept, and would not eat for days. What happened to Emma, should never have happened to a tall, pretty girl from New Haven, from a vine-covered home. I'm sure it's wrong, but I've never been able to get her to talk about it. Long ago she succumbed to its slow, quiet, consummation. I wish I could smoke, but it's a no smoking car. Sometimes I get the feeling she thinks I'm going to leave her. I must get her to talk. On the way out to Versailles, the train made brief stops at Issy-Plaine and Issy-Ville, only local residents going from one suburb to another, got on and off. After a long period of watching the landscape, Emma suddenly turned from the window, bored. She looked for the children; they were safe and happy with the American couple. She pulled out the guidebook from her purse, found a specific page, read something briefly, then put it away. She checked out the noise two seats in front of her. A Greek woman, her aunt, and mother-in-law, and a rather loud family from Argentina were pursuing a lively dialogue. The most interesting part of the conversation was their gropings for language. There was some French, some English, and some Hebrew – the Greek ladies were of Sephardic origin. The conversation lulled and swelled, finally reaching a frenzied pitch with the Argentine father speaking English to the Greek lady's French, the Greek mother-in-law speaking Hebrew to the Argentine mother's listening eyes – she spoke only Spanish, but understood Hebrew – not that they were religious of course, not in the least. In the confusion, the Greek aunt turned her head from side to side, smiling, agreeing to all conversations at once, her hearing aid flipped off. The two, fat adolescent Argentine children whined and complained in Argentine baby talk. And lastly, the Greek lady's silent husband stood by the nearest exit, visibly happy not to be involved.

"As I suspected, we're in line for entrance C. There are two other entrances, A and B."

Emma focused on Paul and her two children who had suddenly re-appeared. She had been concentrating on the palace, trying to figure out where the king and queen's chambers were in relation to the Royal Chapel, but the sun was in her eyes, and her neck burned. She was eager to see the Chapel again, its white columns and arches, with dashes of gold, rising to two stories of elegant proportions. The last time she saw her son Tony he was weaving his way through the clumps of people spread out over the cobblestones, camera around his neck, his arms stretched out as though he were an airplane.

"Are you alright?" Paul asked, leaning towards her.

Emma nodded. He had noticed her neck. She ignored his glance. "I'm fine. You sure about the other entrances?"

"On the east side there's another line that has formed, and it's quite short."

"Why didn't we know about it?" Emma asked, bending down to pick up the lunch bag.

"There are only about 25 people waiting there," Paul assured her. "It's the entrance for guided tours, and it's about two francs more per person."

"You mean there's another way in?" The Coca-Cola T-shirt woman asked, swinging around.

"Yes, on the east side," Paul said.

A few other people turned curiously. Paul continued explaining. "There's yet another entrance to the gardens, and it's free."

"Well for goodness sake," the woman in front of them hurriedly grabbed her husband's arm to get his attention. He was busy talking to someone else.

In no time, Paul was the center of a small hub of people, vacillating as to whether they shouldn't go over to the east side. Emma noticed that the Greek couple from the train were standing beside Paul.

As Paul led them away, he paused a few feet ahead to answer more questions. It was the Americans Penny and Tony sat with on the ride out. The Greek lady told Emma how delighted she was about this other entrance, because her aunt and mother-in-law were suffering terribly with the heat, and they didn't think they would be able to wait in line much longer.

Concerned, Emma turned around to see a swarm of people following them. Paul better be right. As they approached the east side entrance, she had the sudden, uncomfortable feeling that he was wrong. "Paul, maybe that line extends around the building."

"I doubt it, there were just a handful of people clustered around here a few minutes ago."

A sign beside the door said it was for guided tours only. Emma walked around the people to the other side. A neat queue extended for two blocks, beginning behind a sign on the building wall: 'From this point, it will be at least an hour and half before another tour is formed'. Ordinarily, she would have been overcome with anxiety and anger. How many people had they led astray? Again she glanced at the crowd behind Paul, but somehow she felt nothing. The debilitating hives had made her slip into low gear. The only thing remaining was to go into the gardens.

> The kids were fascinated by the formality and layout of the gardens. We walked slowly down the various levels, passing fountains, sculpture and flower beds. We finally stopped to eat lunch at the basin of Apollo. The Sun God in his chariot, overwhelmed both Penelope and Tony, as he rose up from the sea to cast light upon the world, sea monsters and horses struggling in the water. The kids barely touched their cheese sandwiches, then ran around eating yogurt and counting statues, having forgotten their usual rivalries. Emma was very quiet. She was a little

better by lunch, the swelling was subsiding. It had hit while she was waiting in line in the sun, and by the time the kids and I returned to her after checking out the entrances, she was preoccupied and upset. She becomes so nervous and susceptible, she's hardly able to answer questions. The doctors say it's nerves, still because of the baby, and that with time the scars will heal. Two years is a long time. We sat on a bench in the shade under the trees lining the Royal Avenue. I wanted to talk with her, then at lunch, I wanted to talk about things, all kinds of things.

"It looks like nothing has changed around here in years, but it isn't true," Emma said quietly.

"Really?" Paul looked up from his sandwich.

"Did you know that many of the large statues are reproductions?"

"Are you kidding?"

"No, recently they've had to move the originals to the Louvre because of pollution damage. Venus On The Tortoise is there, that's her clone we passed on the North Parterres."

"You could have fooled me."

"Why do you do that?" Emma asked, her words suddenly sharp, her eyes accusing.

"What?" Paul said, retreating, confused.

"Why do you pretend you don't care?" She was angry, her voice high-pitched. "Do you think you're hurting me when you do that?"

"Damn it, Emma, let's not start."

"No really. You've always enjoyed acting as though history and art don't have to be priorities for you, because you're an economist. It's as though you refuse to be moved by what you see, as though your eyes are irrelevant, and, besides, you'll leave the visual things to me – "

"Are you finished?"

"No, but I know you don't want to listen, so I'll stop. I don't want to fight with you."

"Good. Do you want to try getting in again? I could wait in line while you and the kids stay here in the shade."

"No, it's too crowded. If we did get in, we'd probably get caught in a crush somewhere. Mother said the last time she came she was pinned against the doorway between the Mars and Mercury rooms. There was an Oriental group in front of her and Bulgarians behind. She warned me about the crowds. She said I'd find changes. Of course Daddy just laughs at her. He didn't even come with her the last few times, he feels the same way you do about Versailles."

"Emma, I really don't mind trying the line again."

"No. Besides, it's too hot." She shook her head, watching Penelope and Tony help themselves to yogurt from the lunch bag, and then walk over and sit on the fountain's edge.

"What now?"

"I'll come back with them someday, early, so we can be first in line. That should make you happy."

"What?"

Emma shook her head, blinking in the sun. "You thought the whole idea of coming here was stupid."

"Christ Emma, are we going to get into that again? I suppose you're going to tell me that I deliberately took you out of that line."

"No, but I really don't know why you came. Not that it matters now, obviously we can't go inside today. We might as well do the gardens while we're here."

"You mean we can't go in?" Penelope said, licking off her spoon and crushing the yogurt container.

Paul assured her they would come another morning, very early, so they could be first in line. He cleaned up their lunch debris, tucking the plastic spoons into the shoulder bag.

"Do you remember years ago, when we first went to Versailles? Do you Paul?"

"Sure, that summer with Yves."

"We traveled all over France together. What do you think ever became of him? I guess we've lost touch." Emma was deep in thought for a few moments, then continued. "Anyway, do you remember how the three of us sat around after lunch, we ate down by the Petit Trianon, wine and baguettes, paté and cheese. The sun was out, and it was so beautiful. Do you remember?"

"Not exactly, I just remember being here," Paul said.

"It was an extraordinary afternoon," Emma continued. "We talked for a long time, and then a remarkable thing happened. I assumed it happened to the three of us, but perhaps it was just me. I was suddenly aware of an amazing energy, and for a few fleeting seconds, I could read everything in your faces, every line, every pore, every pulse. It was as though the three of us could super-humanly tune in to anything at any level, at the same moment. We seemed to be, for those few moments, interchangeable. We could read each other's minds. It was as though we were being controlled like puppets, and for a second, the strings had become tangled and tied, and we'd all become one, and each other. I realized I loved both you and Yves, and that you both loved me, and each other. I don't think I was ever supposed to understand that."

"I don't remember," Paul said.

"I'm sorry. And I'm sorry our strings never become tangled and tied together anymore," Emma said quietly.

> I guess I must be very tired. Despite the fact that we didn't get in the palace, it was an exhausting day. I hoped the kids felt a little satisfied, I don't think Emma did, although I'm not sure what would have made her happy. I certainly wasn't up to discussing Yves, with his narcissism and bisexuality. Besides, Emma would have denied it vehemently. We'll be back in Paris in about ten minutes. I wonder what we'll do tomorrow? Maybe we'll just go to the Luxembourg gardens and let the kids play at the fountains. As I'm writing this, Emma is awakening. I'll have to put it away. I don't want to explain a journal right now. Her eyes are still closed, but there are tears on her face. I watch her for a few minutes.

"Paul?" Emma opens her eyes.

"Yes Emma?" He put aside the economics book and the journal.

"What did I do wrong?"

"What are you talking about Emma?" he asked, startled, trying to sound matter-of-fact. But she scared him – her voice so odd and eerie – and he hoped his face betrayed no sign of apprehension, fear.

"I've done something very wrong – "

He slid closer and put his arm around his crying wife. "No, no Emma." His words were soothing, but she wept anyway. He rubbed her arm and her shoulders and her back.

"If only I knew what I did – " She pressed her hands to her head, rocking back and forth.

"Emma, Emma, why do you say that? You haven't done anything," he whispered, his voice hoarse with a rush of anxiety and love.

"Then why – "

Emma looked into his eyes, searching anxiously, her own face beyond control, beyond civility.

"Why did that happen to my baby?"

He had no answer. He could not help her. He could only hold her and close out the world, while she struggled with her darkness.

THE MECHANICS OF TURBULENCE IN FLUID

"Then one child is worth a collection of stories, and two children, a novel. What do you think, Jonathan?"

Alex makes her statement, poses her question, hoping to show me she is on task. But her voice is distant, and I cannot imagine where she has wandered, nor what she is thinking. Obviously preoccupied, she bites eagerly into the small tuna sandwich before glancing briefly at the white Conservatory, and then in the direction we'd walked from.

I follow her gaze. Drizzle does not diminish the splendor of Kew Gardens. Flowering plants and shrubs, carefully categorized and labeled, glisten against the black earth and green foliage. The rounded, terraced tops of the large Cedars of Lebanon generously reach out over the cultivated grounds around the brown brick pagoda. I know her eyes, they miss nothing. On this wet day, has she chosen, quite unconsciously, to assess the varying greens, the varying depths of intensities?

She finishes the sandwich and compulsively begins another. Is she really hungry, or just anxious for diversion? Is it the pregnancy? Marriage and Mortimer Glass have made an impact, I decide, envious.

"Jonathan, is all of England so civilized?" She moans quietly.

I shrug. She's sexy, pregnant. Germaine never was. "Alex, are you here?" It's hard to believe I haven't seen her in two years.

"Sorry, I've been so. . . I don't know. . . scattered, I guess. Thoughts come and go. . . sometimes I feel fragmented. All I think about is eating and the baby. Bread, mostly bread. I can't be without it. In the middle of the night, I get up and eat the white stuff, standing at the counter."

Alex reaches for my hand. "Don't be upset Jonathan. I do want to talk about work, and Kew is beautiful," she glances out towards the pagoda, "just like you said. Tell me again, when was it built?"

"1761," I answer.

"It looks like candy, don't you think?" She offers lightly, clearly resisting a sudden, insatiable craving for sugar, as she twirls a strand of dark hair around her little finger. "Red roofs, pink columns and balustrades, red and white trim. I'll bet kids want to eat it." She stares at some school children in yellow slickers, posing on the pagoda's verandah.

"The *Royal* Botanical Gardens?"

She's making an effort to focus, but I don't think she's well. I can feel it. If she told me right now that crazy things are happening to her again, the lows and highs, it wouldn't make any difference. I'd stay with her anyway. Why hasn't she told me? She probably doesn't trust me. I can't blame her.

"Royal, Royal, Royal."

"What are you saying Alex?"

"I'm saying there's not much room left for doubt, is there?" She turns back to me. "Of course they'll be the small uncertainties and mild confusions that surely cross the orderly English mind. But basically, at least here in Kew Gardens, it's quite clear that all's well with England, and has been for a damn long time." She laughs out, anxious to break the seriousness that doggedly accompanies her through life. She refocuses on the table. "The English are great on discretion. Look at the size of these tea sandwiches? You can sit and eat scads, and no one notices. I adore the egg, they put in curry, don't you think?

I watch as she plays with her hair again, the infamous, wavy hair. The first time I saw Alex, the shock was overwhelming. I had seen naked women before, quite a few as a matter of fact, but the incongruity of the scene nearly blew me away. I was in grad school at Iowa, house sitting a professor's place in the country, while he was on sabbatical. Several students had rented the old house next door. They were quite friendly, and kept inviting me to join their parties, but I never did. One fall afternoon, I bumped into Alex and a friend walking hand in hand down the lane. It was a beautiful Indian summer day. The fellow was dressed in dark pants and a hunting shirt. Alex wore walking boots and beige, corduroy jeans, but she was naked from the waist up. Her dark hair streamed around her stunning, white breasts. Alex and her companion smiled, said hi, and kept walking. Later, after we got to know each other, I asked Alex what that had been about. She claimed not to remember the incident, and said she was doing a lot of grass at the time. It took me years to disassociate her hair from her breasts.

If it's possible for a woman's hair to make others stare bitterly into mirrors, suspect their husbands, and launch steamy innuendos into hard facts, this hair had done it. She reaches for another sandwich. Her look hasn't changed; she's still beautiful and it still has nothing to do with the things on her mind. The pale complexion that cannot abide the sun must simply be tolerated. Her eyes, the purple of old, worn bottles washed ashore on Maine coasts, now wear glasses. Men fall recklessly in love with her, children are attracted like magnets to the force of her childishness, and only the most unthreatened of women can befriend Alex. Clearly she has not lost her charm. Is she still as neurotic? I remind myself why I didn't marry her. But I probably should have cast my lot with Alex's instabilities, rather than with Germaine.

"What of three kids, or for that matter, four? Epics, quartets?" She licks some egg filling off the tip of her finger.

"You're asking me?"

Alex pulls the finger out of her mouth. "Of course I'm asking you. You're the expert, you've fathered a few kids in your day." She leans forward, reaching for the tea pot in the middle of the table. "Let's order cakes."

I'm impressed. She has pulled herself out of her dream world, she is functioning. At least that's what she wants me to think. I know you Alex, I know you like the back of my hand. This time you will not deceive me. If you're depressed, I'll know, pregnancy or not. This time, you will not make me feel guilty, I will not leave you. When the time comes, when you need me, I will be with you.

"Jonathan, cakes?"

"Sure, let's order." I must be crazy. What am I thinking? Alex looks wonderful. I can't believe she was ever ill. Besides, she's married now, with a husband, Mortimer Glass. "Well, I may have kids, but I'm not the mother. How pregnant are you Alex? Do you generally eat this much?"

"I'm always famished now. Didn't you notice when I stopped at a bush to eat berries?" She waves one arm vaguely in the direction of some shrubbery. "So what if you weren't the mother, what's that have to do with it? You're a writer and you've had kids. That's what we've been talking about." She pours the tea. "Strong enough?"

"Thanks. I thought we were talking about women. About women having babies and writing. About the amount of time one child takes and the amount of time one collection of stories takes, or a volume of poetry. About – "

"Exactly. That's what we've been talking about."

"Alex, women. Mothers. Primary parents."

"That primary parent stuff doesn't cut it anymore." She stirs her tea, drops in two lumps of sugar, and then pours milk. "Mort agrees with me on that," she says lightly, her eyes closing for a moment, like a bragging child. She turns to the waiter. "Could we have a sweet tray please?"

"Certainly," the waiter says.

His hair is graying, his face is graying, he seems bereft of energy. Tea time in Kew is only a few hours. Does he hold another job, I wonder?

"I'm glad to hear it," I say. "But let me tell you, in the divorce court, the mother is the primary parent."

"Mort and I aren't planning a divorce."

"I'm glad to hear that too." I'm about to tell her there was a time when I wasn't planning one, but I decide against it. Why should I be talking divorce with her? "Alex, it's stopped drizzling. Let's finish eating and walk over to the Palm House. But first tell me about Mort. Tell me everything! I want to hear about a happy marriage."

I've seen Alex only a couple times since we broke up after that Maine summer. We both returned to Iowa for our last year of grad school. I married Germaine, I'd known her for a couple years, and Alex became involved with someone else. At the end of school, I got my first teaching job in Kansas. Alex returned to the East coast. I heard through the grapevine that she wasn't writing much, and was mostly down rather than up; odd jobs, a series of men, and finally a psychiatric ward for a while. Eventually I got a job teaching in the east, Pennsylvania. Two years ago, on one of my visits to New York, I looked her up. She was in the midst of therapy with Mort, and seemed to be getting her life together.

"He's beautiful, Jonathan," she says quietly. "So beautiful... he understands me entirely. Of course he ought to. He was my analyst before we were married." Her voice gains momentum, she speaks confidently. "What can I tell you? We're very happy. We've been together for two years and we're like an old, married couple. I love it."

I don't believe her for a minute. I watch her finish off her tea and pour some more. Alex never wanted to settle down, she never even wanted to be happy.

"I feel so good, I've even joined a music group. What do you think of that? A women's music group! We have solo performers come and play for us – pianists, violinists – then we talk about it."

"My God, that sounds serious Alex!"

"I love it, twice a month I get to feel fenced in and conventional. I even help prepare the refreshments. One old lady taught me not to pour the juice out of the can so fast, and from such a height, because of the mechanics of turbulence in fluid. It splashes. Her husband is a hydraulic engineer."

"Imagine!"

"Stop it Jonathan!"

She's happy, childish. But there are moments of silence before she speaks again, and then her seriousness has returned. "Really, Jonathan, Mort is wonderful. I don't know what I'd do without him." She smooths out the white cloth around her plate. Finally she looks up again. "How's everything on the home front? You seem kind of low."

"Terrible."

"Germaine was always a bitch." Alex says firmly, folding her napkin. "I told you not to marry her. She was jealous of your work." She reaches for my napkin, crumpled beside my plate, and proceeds to smooth and fold it.

"Remember when she tore up your first published story? God, Jonathan, you should have gotten the hint then."

The waiter places a tray of cakes on the table. He's too old to be waiting on tables, and he clearly lost his sense of fun when he lost his dreams, but he smiles bravely, professionally. Alex understands. She tends to understand things like that. Sympathy floods her face, softening, blurring the features. For a moment, the waiter has absorbed her, the rest of her existence must be placed on hold; her emotional expenditures are complete, total. She thanks him, kindly.

"You're probably right," I say. "It hardly matters now. It's over, has been for three months."

"Do you hear from the kids?" Sympathy for the waiter lingers in her voice; it's warm, close.

"I write them, but I'm sure she doesn't give them my letters. When I call, she won't let me speak with them. She lies, says they're out."

"Do you want me to check up on them when I get back? You know, give them a call, take them to the zoo, do some kid stuff?" Her face brightens at the idea.

"You're a strange girl, Alex. I'd love it, but do you think she'd let you near them? My lawyer communicates with them. That's how I know they're alright. Can you believe this? She still makes me feel like a creep. A short, compact, red-headed, red-bearded creep."

"Never mind. How's your work going?"

"Not terrific."

"Why not?" She helps herself to a cherry tart.

"I don't know, I'm bored for the moment, restless."

"You just won the National Book Award, you're on a sabbatical in London, you're free of your wife, and you're bored? You're a turkey, Jonathan."

"And if you weren't pregnant, I'd take you away to a cottage in the Cotswolds."

"I might let you."

"We should have done it in graduate school. How long will you be in town?" I ask.

"Not long enough for that," she laughs. "The baby isn't coming until February, and we're just here a week. Mort has a paper to present at the psychiatric conference."

"Are you writing?"

Alex nods slowly, thoughtfully. "Poetry." She looks longingly at the sweet tray again. "Jonathan," she looks up, "Mort thinks I'm cured of my depressions. Haven't had one for the longest time."

"That's great Alex."

"What do you think?" She presses, testing.

"What do you mean, what do I think? I think it's great. If Mort says you're cured, and you think you're cured, then you must be, right?"

A group of pigeons lift off near the pagoda. We watch without speaking.

"Right." She agrees lightly, pouring more tea. "I want to finish this collection before the baby is born." She pushes some hair behind her ear. "I'm excited about the baby, Jonathan, really I am." She props her elbows onto the table, and sinks her chin into her hands. "Sometimes I worry that afterwards I won't be able to write, or that I might not even want to. Besides I'm pretty old to be a Mama."

"36?"

"37, can't you hear my biological clock?"

"How's your mother?"

"Crazy as ever."

"Somehow," I lean back in my chair, I cross my hands behind my head, "somehow I have trouble visualizing her as a grandmother – sitting on a couch next to a child, reading a story."

"You're not the only one," Alex says, pouring more tea.

"Maybe she can come and help you out when the baby is born. Later, she can train the kid to wait on her hand and foot. That would make her happy."

"Help me? You must be joking? I wouldn't leave her alone in the same room with a kid for ten minutes. Look what she did to me." Alex throws her hands up and shakes her head. "Mother with a child? It's an awesome thought."

We both laugh for a few seconds, then a silence descends.

"What happened to us, Alex? Why didn't it work?"

She shrugs. "God knows we tried."

"We probably should have gotten married. That would have settled it."

"Who knows. No one was getting married in those days."

"Remember the summer we went out to Maine and stayed at my parents' place while they were in Europe? We should have gotten married then. That was good, we should have done it then."

"Sure. You don't remember how we fought, do you? And afterwards – " she shakes her head, "afterwards –" her voice is barely a whisper, she closes her eyes.

"Don't Alex, don't think about it."

Several seconds, then Alex breaks the quiet. "Oh I don't!" She looks at me, her face suddenly confident. "I never think about it anymore. I'm all better now, thanks to Mort! Really I am."

"Good," I say dumbly, lifting my cup. That summer, the last time we fought, I left the house in a fury, and went down to the water. I stayed away for hours. When I got back, she was gone. In my absence she had cut her wrists, and then, fortunately, she'd had the sense to call for help. Unconsciously, I swish the tea around in the cup. 'The mechanics of turbulence in fluid'. I wonder what else Alex learned from the engineer's wife. She's staring out over the garden again, somewhere beyond the pagoda. Her purple eyes, her thoughts, are beyond my reach. I wonder if she's ever tried it again. I hate statistics. About how if you've tried it once, you'll try it again, and again, until you succeed.

The next afternoon, our rendezvous is at Russell Square, a midway point between Alex's hotel and my rooms. Alex brings Mort along, excitedly talking for him, explaining rapidly that he doesn't have to attend the afternoon sessions at the conference. We stand in the square chatting for a few minutes, Alex seemingly in charge of conversation. While she talks, Mort kicks the leaves at his feet, his hands thrust deep into his jean pockets. He's tall, long-legged, and silent. His eyes shift from the leaves to the street, riveting themselves to the passing cars, like a sullen teenager. He's not exactly warm or friendly, and certainly not interested in me. I am glad, however, that Alex is happy, and it's a wonderful October day. When she is done telling me about Mort, we settle on an excursion to the British Museum.

They seem well suited, holding hands as they walk. She isn't at the waddling stage yet. In fact from behind, you wouldn't even know she's pregnant, her hips are still slim, her ass small. She carries a neat little bundle in front. Holding hands with Mort, she looks younger than she is, and I feel envy. Thoughts of Germaine weeping in the courtroom during our divorce trial – her prematurely grey hair, a mad, frizzy halo, her crazed, vengeful eyes – still leave me drained. She continues to puncture my days, cropping up at the strangest times, methodically piercing, leaving holes. I determined last night not to think about Germaine while Alex is in London. She's here for a couple days, and I would like them to be pleasant for both of us.

Mort wants to see the Rosetta Stone. Alex is excited that he expresses interest in something. Despite the terrible crush of people, we stand listening to an elderly man as he translates the English explanation of the Greek, Hieroglyphic and Demotic text into Polish. This historic event is for the sake of one person, his wife, a large, sour-looking old woman with beige cotton socks and a heavy tweed coat. We are left speechless, and today the black slab looks as boring and dull as the old woman. Mort is clearly disappointed.

I take the initiative and lead them through the Egyptian rooms, the Elgin Marbles, the temple of Adelphi, and finally the peace and isolation of the Greek and Roman fragments down in the basement. Not only is Mort silent, but restless, unable to concentrate for long. He stalks off alone, in search of other stimulation, while I point out a colossal marble foot to Alex. A shadow crosses her face as she watches Mort disappear into the next room, so I read to her about the foot and acrolithic statues, those gigantic Roman effigies, bodies of wood, hands, feet and face of marble. I point out that from the toes to the arch there are more than 36 inches. I tell her it was probably to honor the Egyptian god Serapis. I speculate on the height. But I cannot engage her. She says that the word colossus gives her goose flesh.

"I don't think he likes museums very much." Alex murmers. "He gets restless."

"Mort?"

She nods. "He's always working, he isn't used to free time."

"Do you want to go up and look at the manuscripts in the library?" I change the subject.

"No, I think we'd better go."

We find Mort waiting for us outside the fragment rooms.

* * *

The next few hours are spent outdoors, walking and sitting in parks. Clearly I've been wrong about Alex, thinking she might be ill, depressed. Except for her distractibility yesterday at Kew Gardens, she seems happier than I've ever seen her, healthy, calm and looking forward to the baby. Furthermore she appears to be in love with Mort – a realization I find bizarre and difficult to accept – but I do, and am happy for her. As the afternoon unfolds, I find myself sinking into a familiar state of withdrawal. I think of my past, of Germaine. I grieve for my losses; youth, stability, the Pennsylvania farm house I so patiently renovated, my kids I haven't seen in months. The divorce was horrendous, the marriage worse. I can no longer explain away my dejection – a certain thought, a certain event – because lately it trails me relentlessly. I don't deceive myself into thinking I've been happy these last few months, quite the contrary, in fact it's been very difficult in London, much as I love it. I sit here in St. James Park, Alex beside me reading a guidebook – Mort having wandered off to look at the swans in the river – and I'm shocked by my lack of interest and enthusiasm. Mort isn't a barrel of fun, but how much can I blame on him? Alex seems too happy with Mort for any possible rekindling of our flame.

I feel sapped in the afternoon warmth, as though if I sit on the bench long enough, the viscous flesh of my legs, stretched out in front of me, will ooze out of my jeans, above my boots. The afternoon wans. Clouds rush across the sky, shadows elongate, the air cools.

After half an hour of watching Londoners and tourists stroll across the Mall, Alex suddenly turns to me.

"People are always bothering me about my clothes, about the way I dress. Apparently I have no style, no panache."

I see no change, even now that she's pregnant. Muted colors of soft cotton, long and loose, a straw hat. She always dressed like that, I'm not sure what I'm supposed to be looking for. I suppose it could be perceived as quiet, even dull, given that she's a poet. What is she getting at? It's odd to hear her talk about clothes.

"What do you tell them?" I ask.

"I tell them that due to the gross irregularities of my body and spirit, clothes are a hopeless cause on me, so I must go nude. Contrary to the illusions their sight and minds have created, I wear nothing. That shuts them up."

At 5:30, Alex suddenly insists that she wants Indian food, as hot as possible. We have an early dinner, quiet and pleasant, and then a short stroll along Jubilee Walk beside the Thames. Mort walks beside me, his silence thickening the evening air, but I've grown accustomed to him. Actually, I'm grateful I need not make small talk. Flower beds of high, rangy rose bushes, never pruned, line the walkway. The blooms are heady and proud on tall, straggly stalks. The bright lights of the National Theater beam into the dark water. Alex moves a few steps ahead of us, the radiance of her pregnancy – the separateness, the contentment – illuminates the space around her.

The next morning, I'm awakened at eight by phone.
"Jonathan, you awake?"
"Yes, Alex?"
"Jonathan, I think I'm miscarrying."
"What?! My God, the Indian food. Where's Mort?"
"He's at the conference and they can't locate him."
"What's wrong?"
"I'm bleeding all over the bathroom floor. I don't know what to do. It's awful! It's just like the time I – "
"Alex stop. Listen carefully. Can you call the desk for help?"
No answer.
"Alex!"
"I can't, I can't, I can't! It's just like the time I – "
"Look, it'll take me a half an hour to get over to you. I'll call the desk at your hotel and tell them to get a doctor or ambulance, something. Hang on Alex."
"I'm scared Jonathan."

By the time I arrive at the hotel, the ambulance has already come and taken Alex away. I have to listen to the desk clerk tell me all about the blood in the bathroom, and pandemonium amongst the cleaning staff, before he tells me the name of the hospital.

"St. Thomas'." He finally offers.

The taxi takes forever, and I keep wondering if I shouldn't be trying to contact Mort, but I decide it's important for someone to be with Alex immediately. If she loses the baby it will be devastating for her. It will set her back incredibly.

I pay the cabbie and hurry up the hospital steps. It's crowded and drafty inside, and I have to wait in line at the information desk.

"You've just admitted a Mrs. Alexandra Glass. I believe she was having a miscarriage. Could you tell me how she is, and can I see her?"

The woman behind the desk looks down at a clipboard with lists of names. Her pencil stops at Alex's. She looks up frowning.

"Are you the husband?"

"No, no just a friend."

"Well, under the circumstances, we need to get a hold of the husband, in this case."

"Yes, yes I know, but I'm a good friend, she'll want to see me. You see I'm the one she called when she began aborting – "

"Aborting?" The woman says.

"Yes, when she started bleeding on the bathroom floor – "

"It doesn't say anything about aborting." The woman glances down at her clipboard again. "No, Mrs. Glass is not aborting – "

"Thank God," I breathe deeply.

"It says here," the woman checks again, shakes her head, "it says here she's cut her wrists."

A GENTLE MADNESS

In the middle of February, Annie Hume went mad. The doctor called it a nervous breakdown. Her friend Kate called it insanity. It happened on what seemed to be a perfectly normal winter Thursday of her life. Annie had washed laundry and hung it out on the drying racks around the wood stove. Upstairs she had tried to tidy as best she could, but it was hard, with the dirt of past generations still unattacked by the uncertain, young Humes. She had fixed the girls' toy elephant, she had even made peanut butter cookies, probably nursing Angelina while the margarine softened. Annie tried to be a good mother, she worked at it. But at that point in the winter, the Hume house and the four Hume children continually smelled of burning wood, old wallpaper, and the stale, purple velour couch and armchair that Annie had purchased at an auction.

Kate had dropped by to visit Annie only days before, and she had noticed how grubby the children looked. They climbed all over in felt slippers like little monkeys in search of a resting place; a table top, a bureau, the back of a couch, anywhere they could crouch and suck their thumbs, their yellow hair, fine and straight, their bright eyes blinking shyly like their father's. Kate hadn't wanted to think about it, but Annie did seem unusually nervous and flushed, unable to concentrate, hardly speaking. On that Thursday, Annie had taken care to put wood in the furnace, and something in the oven for dinner. The baby was asleep when she'd gone upstairs to put away linen, when something snapped, when she sat down in the darkened closet, and began counting sheets.

Martin Hume found her there when he returned home from his twelve-hour shift at the nuclear power plant. The house had cooled down; the three older children had fallen asleep in front of the T.V., the baby still sleeping in her crib. Annie was sitting cross-legged on the floor of the closet, staring straight ahead, smiling, piles of sheets and bedding around her.

The neighbors were very good. They came around eager to help out, until Annie's mother, Irene, could come down from where she lived, Lamb's Way. She moved in immediately and set to work caring for the children and the house. She was a small energetic woman, with black hair and lively eyes. She always wore navy-blue nylon slacks and tops, covered with little bits of lint and snags. She was an incessant smoker, a cigarette accompanied her everywhere. Kate had met her on several occasions before, and it struck her as odd that such a positive and confident little lady could have raised such a vulnerable girl.

Martin Hume divided his time between his twelve-hour shifts at Point 200-H and the county hospital in Trollmount. It meant a lot of driving. Kate knew that at the best of times Martin Hume was not much of a talker. He was a silent, shy young man; Annie had generally done the talking, explaining and apologizing. If he did talk, it was the odd remark about the weather, and if it was summer, about the haying. He was trying to make a go of the two fields he owned, but it wasn't easy, working long shifts at the Point. After what happened to Annie, Martin became impossible. Kate tried calling him a couple times a week when he returned from a visit to Trollmount. He seemed to have absolutely no news at all of Annie. One morning, Kate spoke with Irene on the phone. Irene told her to drop by because she had been to see Annie.

Later that afternoon Kate sat at the kitchen table listening to Irene. She could hear the children playing in an upstairs bedroom, the baby, no doubt, in the crib. It was Martin's day off. He lay on the couch along the west wall of the kitchen reading *Time* magazine. Although he was in his stocking feet, he wore his outdoor jacket. Kate imagined he had stepped out for the mail and some wood for the stove. As he pulled *Time* out of the box, no doubt he immediately became engrossed. She could picture him walking slowly down the lane back to the house, his face buried in the magazine. When she entered the kitchen and greeted Martin, he had looked up and nodded, then dropped his face to his reading. Kate noticed that Irene had washed and ironed the plaid blanket from the kitchen couch. It looked remarkably clean. In fact, the whole house looked refreshingly tidy under Irene's management.

"I had a chance to go to the city," Irene said, drawing deeply on her cigarette. Her face had grown tired and sallow while she'd been caring for Annie's family.

She tilted her head up and exhaled a long puff of smoke. "My niece Gracie got a notion to do some shopping in Trollmount, but she had to head home by noon. Her mother-in-law took that spell a couple nights before, and Gracie had to be back in time for chores at her father-in-law's. Dairy farmers," Irene explained, reaching over her cup, aiming her cigarette towards the old saucer on the middle of the table. "Turns out the hospital don't even want visitors until two." She tapped the ashes carefully, slowly. Leaning towards Kate, she lowered her voice. "Martin just forgot to tell me. He's got so much on his mind." She glanced over at her son-in-law and shook her head. "I feel real sorry for the boy, it must be an awful worry." She straightened up in her chair, picking at the lint on her sleeve.

"I said to Gracie, so supposing I have to wait around, it won't kill me." She rubbed out the remains of her cigarette. "Gracie felt awful bad. Anyway, that's how I come to take the bus back."

Irene had another sip of coffee, then pulled the pack of cigarettes closer. "I did get to see Annie though." She reached into the neck of her jersey and pulled out a book of matches. "The kids you know," she flashed the matches secretly, "I don't like leaving them around."

"You can't be too careful," Kate agreed.

"I found her doing pretty good," Irene said cheerfully, lighting a cigarette. "Of course," she hesitated, inhaling deeply, "it'll be a while yet before she's all better." She stared silently at her cup, then looked up at Kate. "It was real nice of the neighbor lady Mrs. Mullin. She came in and stayed with the family so I could go to Annie. I've just gone the once. Don't you think it's more important that Martin be going down, than me?"

Kate nodded reassuringly.

"Truth is, I've been worried about Annie since the last baby." Irene shook her head. "By times she's awful low, just plain sad, like she don't even want to talk." She lowered her voice again, her face intense, as though she strained to remember something. "Bad nerves, ever since she was a kid," Irene said, lifting a bit of tobacco off the tip of her tongue. "When she was little, everything frightened her, what with the older kids teasing her the way they did." Irene became pensive again. "Maybe I spoiled her too much, being the baby and all . . ."

"Nonsense," Kate sympathized. "Did the doctor say it would be alright for Annie to have visitors?"

Irene nodded. "I know she'd be awful pleased to see you. She's always telling me about you and your husband and the kids, and how kind you've been. I really appreciate it."

Kate smiled, finishing her coffee. Before she left, she arranged with Martin that she would accompany him on his next visit.

The hospital in Trollmount was a large, red brick institution, spreading out for what seemed to be several blocks. It was situated on the outskirts of town, and set back in a large, lawn-like area, devoid of any niceties like perennials or trees or shrubs. Only an officious, empty flower bed faced the front entrance. Petunias, Kate decided, thinking of the long summers and how petunias required no care. The drive down had not been unpleasant, though relatively silent. The sun was out, and the roads were snowless and dry. Kate felt sorry for Martin. So many minutes of every day seemed terribly awkward for him. She realized Annie's illness had been an indescribable shock, but he could not bring himself to discuss her, or for that matter, to discuss anything. Had he always been this silent with Annie? God help her if he had.

They had to wait outside the ward doors for about fifteen minutes. Martin's gray eyes watched as the doctors and nurses and carts went by. Nothing he saw altered his features. He was in his late twenties, but there was a resigned, uninvolved look on his face. It was as if he had come to the conclusion that he never had been, and never would be a participant, merely an observer. Kate felt disheartened. She waited silently with Martin until the doors were finally opened. After the nurses came out carrying covered, stainless steel basins, Kate and Martin were allowed to enter.

If Martin and Annie had problems communicating before, on that day it was impossible. Despite the fact that it was the middle of winter, large fans droned incessantly. Kate had heard two nurses talking about a failure in the heating system for that wing; they were waiting for the repairmen. The other eight or nine women in the ward seemed to jabber or cry or sigh ceaselessly. Annie sat in a rocking chair in the corner, humming to herself. She did not see them approach. Once they stood before her, her eyes flickered for a second, acknowledging their presence, briefly, and then promptly retreated. She seemed quite content, rocking away, pretending she was alone.

Martin greeted her, bending over, gently running two fingers down the side of her face. She did not look up.

"Feeling a bit better today, Annie?" His voice croaked, hoarse and tight.

There was no response.

How he must hate to see her dressed like that, Kate thought, glancing at the blue hospital gown and the corduroy slippers hanging from her limp, white legs. Annie's hair was dirty and hung around her pale, blank face. Was she on medication, Kate wondered? No doubt. They all looked drugged, Kate decided. Irene hadn't mentioned anything about drugs, but she had said the doctors told Martin he must come as often as he could. Annie would have to talk about it all, so she could understand why it had happened.

When Martin gave up and stepped back, Kate squatted down in front of Annie for a few moments, trying to catch her eyes. She could not. Finally she simply took her hands; they felt dry and scaly, neglected. Then, for some odd reason, she told Annie the children were alright, and not to worry about them. Kate stood up. Later she wondered why she had mentioned the children? What made her think Annie was worried about them?

Martin looked around the room uncomfortably. Kate saw that the other women were much older than Annie, some quite haggard and worn. Their loose bodies flopped around under their bathrobes.

"You have to go now. That bell means it's dinner time." Annie bent over to scratch her ankle as she spoke. She straightened up again. A flush of color had spread over her cheeks from bending, but her eyes were the same, dull, blank. She stood up and tightened the belt on her chenille bathrobe. They could see the laundry stampings on her nightgown.

"You have to go," she said again, scratching and peering at something on her elbow.

"Don't you want to come home, Annie?"

Kate heard the bewilderment in Martin's voice.

"Maybe," Annie said, distracted, still staring at her elbow. Martin leaned forward and kissed his wife on the forehead. "I'll come again soon," he whispered, his eyes closed. With that, he turned abruptly and headed towards the door.

Kate reached over and patted Annie's arm. "Get better soon, Annie. We all miss you."

It wasn't until Martin and Kate were opening the ward doors that they heard Annie cry out after them. When they turned, her lips were not moving. Her scared face was pale and lost in the large room.

LILLY AND BRUNO

"How much more are the preferred seats?" It was a simple enough question, at least it appeared so to Lilly.

"How many do you want?"

"Three," Lilly replied, "but first I want to know how much more the preferred seats are."

"Fifteen for the lot of you."

She heard him ripping off the tickets.

"Please, I want to know what the difference is, how much more – " Lilly was suddenly shoved forward, her chest hit the counter ledge. On her left, an impatient female voice hissed, "ya gonna take all day?!"

"Lady, you want the tickets or not?"

Without further discussion, she slid her money cautiously across the counter, fingers extended. Momentarily confused, she didn't know whether to be pleased or angry that the ticket man hadn't realized, and he hadn't, it was quite obvious. She had come prepared for the crowds and the jostling and the noise, but somehow she hadn't counted on the ticket man being rude. She'd thought he'd be especially polite, but then if he hadn't realized, how could she expect–

"The entrance, Aunt Lilly, it's this way!"

Breathing deeply, still holding onto the children and her bag, Lilly turned in Annie's direction.

"This way, come on!" Annie called again, leading.

Braving the elbows and swinging bags and banner sticks, Lilly pushed and pulled with the children, three boats tossed at sea. She felt great determination. Despite the autumn chill, nervous excitement had made her warm, her heart beating as though a squirt of novocaine had accidently found a vein.

Lilly had left the house with her usual caution, feeling tight and uncertain, one hand gripping Annie's, the other grasping David's little arm. They'd taken a bus all the way into the heart of the city, then changed to a #32 that would deliver them out to San Geronimo Mall. The circus had set up in the vast spread of land beyond the mall parking area, under the dizzy cloverleaf junction of Interstate 40 and Loop 210. She'd managed very well after all, so there had been no need for her younger sister Rose to carry on the way she had last night.

"Are you certain you'll be alright?" Rose had fretted as she'd let the dishwater out of the sink. "Are you sure you can manage this? After all, Lilly, the last time you went to a circus – "

"Please, Rose, please don't go on about it!" She had desperately wanted to do it, to carry it through. It wasn't a question of taking the children on an outing, she'd done that often enough. It was the fact of the circus. She'd often thought about it, about the day the posters would appear on the telephone poles, and the children would come to her, pleading to go. Of course they knew nothing about their Aunt Lilly and another circus, or about fate or loneliness. They knew only that their Aunt Lilly would take them, and they were right. It was time, she could do it, she would. Besides, she loved listening to David's talk about everything he saw.

"Well, at least Annie's getting to be a big girl," Rose had said resolutely, washing out the sink. "She'll help you," she added softly.

As Lilly had reached for the last dish to dry, she'd felt the gentle pat of her sister's damp hand.

Rose had been good to her, taking her in the way she had two years ago, after Mama died, insisting that 'no sister of hers was going to live in one of those places.' Mama passed away just after Rose's divorce, so the timing couldn't have been better. Lilly had often wondered if maybe Mama hadn't worked out some contract with God concerning the timing of events. She wouldn't put it past her. Mama had always felt confident about her communications with God, and besides, she knew a lot about contracts. She'd been top legal secretary over at Finch, Finch and Hollands ever since Lilly could remember, and it had been through Mama that Lilly had gotten her job. After the funeral, and after Rose had disposed of the house, Lilly had simply walked down the two blocks, and moved in with Rose and the children. She'd brought her savings with her, to pay her way of course, but times were getting harder than they'd ever been. Ends just met in that little house on J Street, cold in the winter, hot in the summer.

On muggy, summer evenings, Rose and Lilly sat out on the wooden veranda, Rose talking softly of moving uptown to one of the suburbs, Lilly silently sipping her iced tea. While Rose compared Tanglewood Trails to Camelot 1, Lilly knew that her sister's pretty, preoccupied face stared out past the scrap of lawn, past her children playing in the street, past reality. Listening to Rose and the sounds of the neighborhood, Lilly remembered their own mother worrying about the same streets, the same problems, the same boarded up stores and bars only blocks away. But Rose's dream seemed to be slipping further and further away. The endless series of clerking and secretarial jobs, the money Joe gave her for the children, and even the rest of Lilly's savings, all of it would not add up to Tanglewood Trails. It would take a miracle, and Rose knew it. Yet with what optimism she pushed on, with what kindness she always stated that she didn't know where she would be without Lilly.

Lilly did try to make herself useful. She was able to do laundry and prepare supper and be home for the children after school. But in fact, she'd never be able to manage on her own, and truth be told, she was almost always frightened. She'd worried a great deal before she'd fallen asleep last night. The mere fact of where the bus would let them off, and how far a walk it was to the ticket booth, and afterwards, taking the correct bus home again, all that had caused her to lay awake for over an hour. Nevertheless, she was determined.

They stepped from the cool air into the dankness of popcorn and straw and sweat. It was as crowded inside the tent as out, and far noisier. The band up above their heads was warming up. Two separate voices nearby called out about souvenir program books, warning that this was the last chance, they would not be offered once the show began. Was she over cautious Lilly wondered, holding tightly to David's hand? While they were waiting in line at the gate of the tent, how many times had she asked David if his jacket was buttoned, and Annie if her ears were covered, reminding her of her recent infection? How many times had she re-adjusted her own sweater, and checked to make sure her bag was zipped? She had always been like that, wanting certainty and control in her life. She'd never felt comfortable with the element of chance or the unknown. That was one thing the accident had not changed, she had simply become more so. Even when she went shopping with Rose, she insisted that Rose memorize the car's position in the mall parking area. Lilly couldn't bear to be part of the departure pandemonium, with the shopping bags, and the children upset because they were tired, and there she stood, helpless, while Rose scurried about, asking people if they'd seen a beige Chevy.

"Look what they're selling here Aunt Lilly!" David was pulling her in another direction. The smell of rubber toys and candy floss mingled with the heat of the popcorn machines.

"It's all junk, David."

"How do you know?" David demanded.

"Come on David, we have to find our seats!" Annie called excitedly, leading them towards the bleachers. "We have green tickets, so I think we're in this section." She paused for a moment. "I wonder what box seats are Aunt Lilly?"

"Do they have box seats too?" Lilly sked, surprised.

"Yes, right down in the front, and they're chairs, not bleachers, but you have to have red tickets for that section," Annie said, glancing up at the signs above the divided sections.

"The ticket man didn't tell me about box seats or I would have – "

"It doesn't matter, Aunt Lilly, our seats will be just fine. We have to climb up two bleacher rows, okay? Come on," Annie tightened her grip on Lilly's hand.

Lilly felt bad. If she'd known, she would have been willing to get the box seats, considering the children had never been to the circus, and that she herself hadn't been in years. Ten, to be exact, that time with the girls from Finch, Finch and Hollands. She certainly would have been willing to get box seats, Lilly thought, perturbed.

"Right here, Aunt Lilly, we can see very well from here. There, are you comfortable?"

Lilly nodded, re-adjusting herself. She felt Annie's hands on her feet.

"Put your feet on the bleachers in front of you."

"Perfect!" Lilly smiled.

It was out of the question to drag back outside to the ticket booth, it was too late. Lilly could feel the tent filling up. There were people both behind and in front of her. David's little body was close beside her.

"Can you see well, David?" she asked, turning.

"Yup, when will it start?"

"Soon," Lilly said, patting his knee. "Just as soon as everyone is in."

"There's a clown selling programs," Annie said, "I'm going to get one before it starts. Be right back."

Finch, Finch and Hollands – had it really been that long, ten years? Yes, Annie was days old, Rose was still in the hospital with her.

"I'm back, and look, the master of ceremonies! It's starting!"

"Ladies and gentlemen, children, welcome, welcome to – "

"Why is he wearing that fancy hat?"

"Just watch, David, in a minute everyone in the circus is going to come out in parade," Lilly whispered, bending down to David.

With great fanfare from the band, Lilly quickly sensed the spectacular pomp and splendor of the parade; the children were enthralled. The ringmaster's microphoned words called out over the piercing music, the clapping and whistling. The occasional call of an animal broke through the noise. Lilly could feel the pounding heat of the large spotlights. It took only a comment from Annie about a costume, or one of David's cues, and Lilly was off.

"The elephants!"

Ten years ago, it had been on a lark that they'd gone to the Ringling Brothers' performance, she and the girls from Finch, Finch and Hollands. They were in the habit of going out together every Saturday night, and that specific evening, there was nothing good at the movies, and none of them felt like bowling. All four of them were in their mid-thirties, and all four still hadn't managed to catch husbands. Lilly had never considered her tall, large-boned frame unattractive, it was more a question of shyness and fear of change. Besides, the only men who ever asked her out were those tired, damp-looking clerks from the shipping office across the hall. She really preferred going home to watch T.V., even with Mama.

Despite that Mama had been a legal secretary and knew about contracts, she hadn't been a very liberated lady. She had named her daughters Lilly and Rose after the Currier and Ives print that had hung in the parlor since the beginning of time. Mama did not approve of unescorted girls at the circus – it was different than the movies – an unescorted girl was, to put it plainly, vulnerable. Lilly had gone anyway, laughing that she was a far cry from that pale, fragile Currier and Ives Lilly, holding her flower, smiling demurely. In the years that followed, it had taken Lilly a long time to get over her anger and confusion. How was it possible that Mama had known her better than she knew herself?

"Aunt Lilly, the elephants!" David repeated.

Lilly gratefully patted her nephew's knee and reached for his little hand. She conjured up images of shimmering, bare elephant girls, gyrating on those gray masses as their clumsy beasts swayed down the hippodrome, trunks connected to tails like cut-out paper dolls. Pegasus, with his white, cardboard wings, neighed as he threw back his spectacular white body, lifting his front legs over the clouds of dry ice smoke. The sole, white llama wore a silvery, blue poncho and marched behind the array of horses with their braided, ribboned manes. There was always a stupid little dog, dressed like a clown, running off somewhere, confused. David told her of the jugglers and the dog act and the clowns. Annie told her of the gymnastic German twins and their golden sleigh, outfitted with bars and rings and other acrobatic paraphernalia. At both ends of the sleigh, from two large, lit globes that pulsed on and off, the girls' tiny, unnatural, upside down bodies balanced perfectly on miniscule pinkies. The air in the tent became muggy and close.

"And now folks, for the act you've all been waiting for, please welcome – "

"It's the trapeze people!" Annie shrieked. "Look at their capes and hats and gloves! Aunt Lilly, look! At the bottom, the capes are lined with plastic!"

"That's so they won't get dirty, Annie. They have to drag through a lot of straw and stuff at each performance."

"Because of the risks involved in the next act, ladies, gentlemen and children, we ask that everyone remain absolutely silent. Please note that this act will be performed without the aid of a net."

Lilly could still see him, every detail, as though he were standing down in the ring at this very moment, as though the clock had been turned back ten years. She had found the atmosphere of overt sex overwhelming, and her own desire, sudden and choking. Lilly had never experienced anything like it. Swift and total, all else fell away instantly; the girls from the office, her caution, the animals, the performers. Never before had she wanted anything as she wanted him. He was broad and dark and extraordinarily well built, extraordinarily over-sexed. Most likely he was a foreman, one of those in charge of hoisting up the poles and rolling down the massive tents. He was king compared to the awkward, slow-moving circus sweeper. The unblessed soul who perpetually trips on the ring's edge, as he stumbles to clean up after the elephants. While some remarkable feat takes place in the maze of wires above his head, the poor man looks out for more dung.

"Look Aunt Lilly, he let go!"
"Watch, David, he'll catch the other man's hands!" Lilly whispered.
Silence, then music, clapping and shouts of delight.
"How did you know, how could you tell?" David gasped, surprised.

Bruno's precision was as high as the performers. He looked like a Bruno, a man who in his past had committed a crime of passion. The possibilities had seemed infinite as Lilly watched him move around the ring, performing his various tasks like a well-fed, well-oiled animal. Without a doubt, he had spent the better part of his youth incarcerated in a high risk penal institution. After that, the circus.

Bruno, hands behind his back, waited patiently for his cue; a swinging rope he must grab and hold taut, the discarded balancing pole that must be caught, or finally, a quivering elbow in need of steadying, as a spinning, sparkling, female figure suddenly drops to a standing position after the trapeze's dizziness. With Bruno's swift, confident grip of the woman's elbow and forearm, the world knew, and Lilly knew, that they were lovers, that smiling, posed, panting blond and Bruno.

Lilly and the Finch girls had gotten the best box seats. They were so close to the action and lights she was sure she could hear the blond's exhausted panting. Lilly felt a blush spread across her neck and face. Teeming undercurrents of sex and deviation, jealousy and bitterness, steamed up from the straw like the odors of the circus. Was it her imagination, the flesh and bleached hair, the feathers and glitter, the music, trampling, and stomping? It was as though the hippodrome were the lid of an enormous, seething vessel of iniquity, continually bubbling.

Lilly leaned forward, spellbound. If only – she would give anything to be that blond girl standing next to him, one of his hands on her elbow, the other in the small of her back. Anything –

"Lilly, you had enough?" The Finch girls were standing, waiting.

"What?" Lilly turned towards them.

"We're bored, you coming? We're going out somewhere to get a drink. Coming?"

"No, go ahead, I'll stay and take the bus home." How could they leave? Had they not noticed Bruno? Was she the only one?

"She was spinning from her teeth, Aunt Lilly, it was terrible, but now she's down." Annie sighed, relieved.

"Is there a man in blue overalls standing next to her, holding her arm and elbow?"

"Yes, but how did you know?" Annie asked.

"They have to have someone. She's probably pretty dizzy, and if she weren't being held, no doubt she'd fall."
"I suppose so," Annie said.
"What does he look like?"
"Who, Aunt Lilly?"
"The man in blue overalls, is he dark?"
"No, he's blond, why?"
"No reason, just wondering," Lilly replied quietly.

Afterwards, after the Finch girls had left, and after the performance was over, Lilly was possessed with a burning desire to see Bruno. It wasn't a question of talking with him, chatting, becoming acquainted. She just wanted to be near, maybe touch him; she wanted to see what color his eyes were, and if he had a scar on his face, considering his past of crime. She knew it was ridiculous, she knew what her mother would say, she knew how the Finch girls would laugh and carry on if they found out. Lilly didn't care, she was determined to find him.

When the last of the audience disappeared from the circus grounds, the outside spotlights were dimmed. Lilly lurked self-consciously around the ticket booth, hoping to see him, watching the workers go about their jobs with props or animals or costumes. The darkness did not seem to bother them. Finally she began walking around, looking for blue-overalled men. Lilly had trouble in the dark, straining, stumbling. She asked one of the clowns where Bruno's trailer was.

"Bruno? There ain't no Bruno here. I'm Jim-Bob, will that do?" He smiled.

Lilly recognized the lion tamer and the Chinese elephant girl going into a trailer. Feeling reckless with determination, she peered at each man she passed, but still no Bruno. Finally it occurred to her to inquire after the young trapeze actress, the spinning, panting blond. A fat lady, sitting alone with a dog in her lap, told her the blond's trailer was the last one, on the edge of the encampment.

Lilly started towards it. She passed a midget leaning against a trailer door. He winked at her. She recognized the master of ceremonies coming towards her; he was wearing an undershirt, carrying a bucket of water. Lilly was certain Bruno would be with the trapeze girl. She had absolutely no idea what she was going to say to him when she found him.

As she hurriedly approached the trailer, Lilly had to step over some large, steel poles lying on the ground. In her anxiety, she miscalculated her steps. Her foot caught, she felt herself fall.

Three days later in the hospital, Lilly still couldn't see anything. The doctors couldn't say for sure whether she'd ever regain her sight, she'd had a bad blow to her head. For a while after the accident, she'd had amnesia. In that time, she used to ask her mother over and over again to tell her what happened after she'd fallen. She knew the story by heart. The master of ceremonies was the first to find her. The fat lady ran for the trapeze girl and Bruno, thinking they knew Lilly, since she'd been asking about them. The trapeze girl called for an ambulance while Bruno stayed with her. Lilly knew he called the hospital twice, before the circus left town. By the time she regained consciousness, Bruno was long gone. Although she eventually regained her memory, she was never able to remember anything about the accident. And of course, her sight never returned.

"Aunt Lilly, look!" David shouted, "the lion tamer is starting a fire in the lion's cage!"

THE NAPOLEONIC WARS

Because it was Friday and the Rare Book Room would be closed over the weekend, Norah Banning pulled the dark library drapes and adjusted the special humidifier before turning out the lights. Out in the hall, once the double glass doors were locked and double checked, she fumbled into her coat, her face drawn and preoccupied. It had been an unusually distressing day, Norah reassured herself, searching for a grocery list in her pocket. Exhaustion had caught up with her. One unpleasant thought had led to another, and now she found herself down, rather than up, fighting off familiar confusions: her seventy-nine year old mother, the recent years of strained relations with her own daughter Toby. Norah stared at the grocery list in her hand. This fall, thank God, Toby was away at university.

   Norah pulled herself together. Tucking away her list, she started briskly down the hall towards the elevator, re-confirming certain established facts. For the last fifteen years she'd been walking to work, mid-western weather permitting. The occasional loose slabs of cement, cowering under the smart cracking of her brisk heels, served as reminders of where she was, lest she forget. But Norah Banning still considered herself a pavement-loving New Yorker. In a fine canvas bag, she carried her umbrella and her lunch: a piece of fruit and a slab of imported cheese between two slices of homemade herb bread. Her suits were of the best tailored wool and her shirts of linen or silk. Her thin, muscular legs felt only the sheerest quality hose.

Without fail, her wavy black hair was immaculately cropped at the nape of her neck. These were the facts. But in the face of upset, in the face of a bad day, they were not particularly helpful.

The day wasn't over yet, Norah realized, crossing the main lobby of the library. She still had to pick up her mother at the airport; she still had to host the history department. If the day had been Eric's instead of hers, Norah knew he would have found it all vaguely trying, but certainly nothing to cause the stress that she had been through. But then, that was why he had been made Dean of Humanities, and, of course, that was also why she had married him.

An hour later Norah silently unloaded the groceries onto her kitchen counter. With her coat still on, she folded and put away the paper bags, listening to the muffled upstairs sounds. Eric was having his bath. Norah frowned, thinking again of the afternoon and the young girl who had walked into the Room. She was still upset, the sheer coincidence of it. It's said that everyone has a twin somewhere, but this was incredible. A complete quirk of nature.

She couldn't even remember her name, Norah thought. It didn't matter. What mattered was that the girl looked remarkably like Eric's Lise. From the beginning of the business with Lise, Eric had neglected telling Norah one thing. Of course he had spoken of everything else: of Lise's talent and sensitivity, of how she was not an ordinary student, not an ordinary young writer, of how the rest of the faculty seemingly had dismissed her as mad. But what he had neglected telling Norah, was how breathtakingly beautiful the girl was. At the time, Eric and his compassionate nature were approaching forty-five, somewhat tired and disillusioned. That magical combination of extraordinary talent and the pathetic inability to cope with life had once again charmed her husband. Thinking about it, Norah was certain she could feel the vibrations of her staled jealousy.

Of course, nothing, absolutely nothing had happened. She knew that now. In a sense, she'd known it at the time; but she'd felt so useless, and consequently, she'd behaved childishly. After Lise had perched herself on the window ledge in the womens' bathroom – third floor, English department – and had threatened to jump, Eric took on the burden of her cause single-handed. Norah had wanted no part of the project. Eventually there was some form of recovery for Lise. The years that followed brought Lise's manuscripts in the mail as steadily as Norah's *New York Times*. On Norah's part, there was remorse, or something resembling it.

All this because of a quirk of nature, Norah thought, looking over the cheese and crackers, the mixers and tonics that lay across her counter. Bending down to put away some cans under the sink, Norah suddenly wondered whether the history people would all come tonight. Not that it mattered really. The faculty gatherings that she had begun with her usual unharnessed energy – soirées for better communications and understanding – had turned into useless, boring, perfunctory affairs. Eric of course, had been patiently dubious from the start. She pushed the old juice can filled with bacon fat to the back and adjusted the tin foil cover. She stacked a few cans. It smelled stale under the sink; the potatoes were sprouting again.

"*The Napoleonic Wars*," the girl had said, popping a lifesaver into her mouth, "with the original etchings."

After Norah had overcome her initial shock, she realized it was the girl's eyes that had been so like Lise's; cool and defiant. A handknit, Bolivian cap, dirty and multicolored, was pulled down over her head; the round face, pale, almost angelic. Striped overalls pulled tautly across her pregnant belly. Of course Lise hadn't been pregnant. At that very moment, it had struck Norah that the hat, as well as its bearer, must surely have just descended mountains, and still not found water.

"They're on the second shelf above the reserve table," Norah had said politely, still awed. She had watched uncomfortably as a grubby hand pulled off the cap and a mass of long black hair appeared, dampish and untidy.

"Please sign here." Norah had handed the girl a reserve slip with the usual information.

The girl reached for a pencil from Norah's desk and immediately put it into her mouth. As she read over the slip, she chewed the pencil, appearing to study the piece of paper as she might a will. Finally she signed.

In her distraction and confusion, Norah had filed *The Napoleonic Wars* reserve slip in the wrong place. Then she'd walked over to the girl as though to say something to her. For a few seconds she stood there staring down at the enormous book spread on the table, at the knit cap, at the face. Then she'd walked back to her desk, feeling quite defeated. It wasn't like her she realized, straightening up to the sink. What had she intended to say to the girl? Norah looked again at the groceries on the counter. Some of the history wives probably wouldn't come. One could never be sure though. Last week when she'd sat under the hairdresser's scissors, she'd overheard someone say that Dean Banning was one of the only ones left who still had gatherings with a bar instead of punch. Norah carried the cheese to the refrigerator.

"Not again!" Eric Banning stood in the kitchen doorway. His hands were thrust deep into his bathrobe pocket, the newspaper tucked under one arm.

Norah looked up from the opened cheese bin. He looked comfortable and warm. "Have you forgotten?" She could tell he had. "History tonight." She closed the bin, straightened up and closed the refrigerator.

Eric sighed loudly.

He was probably looking forward to a quiet evening, Norah realized, taking off her raincoat. She wondered if he remembered that her mother was arriving that evening.

"How many more?" Eric asked, walking over to the counter. He put down the paper and opened a box of crackers.

"We've done the English department, Art and Music, Philosophy and Religion. . . ."

"Do you think all deans do this?" He pouted, biting into a sandwich of three crackers.

"Only the conscientious ones," Norah said softly. She could feel a slight smile cracking her face like a shell. Was she that tense? She walked over to the coat closet.

"Next year," Eric mumbled, "next year. . . ."

"I'll remind you not to be so conscientious," Norah called back, as she hung up her coat and re-entered the kitchen.

"Hard day?" He asked quietly, placing his hand on the back of his wife's neck.

Norah remained silent for a moment.

"After you left home this morning, the day got better, I hope?" He smiled.

"I was awful to Mr. Gantz," Norah mumbled. "He wanted to talk about the first edition of *Pamela* again. I wish he'd finish his dissertation."

"What else happened?" Eric asked, his eyes gently probing his wife's face.

"Nothing. A few other people were in. A young girl who. . .do you feel like chops or liver?" Norah asked suddenly, turning back to the refrigerator.

"A young girl?" Eric repeated, waiting.

Norah nodded and looked at her husband. "She reminded me of Lise, ten years ago."

Eric remained silent for a few moments. "Chops," he said. "Was she pregnant and wearing overalls?" He smiled.

Norah looked at her husband in disbelief. She touched her head. "A little hat?"

He nodded. "She was one of the representatives of the student demonstrators. She sat in my office for an hour this morning, nodding and bitching and eating lifesavers."

"Incredible," Norah said. Somehow Eric always managed; problems were always solved. At times, it was just the matter-of-fact tone of his voice. Or perhaps, it was what he said, calmly, thoughtfully. Regardless, she always felt herself more relaxed, relieved. It was odd that they should have both seen her on the same day – "Did anything come of the meeting?" Norah asked, taking the package of meat out of the refrigerator.

"No, but it managed to remind me of Lise's manuscript that I've had for weeks and still haven't read."

"Could you get to it this weekend?" Norah asked sympathetically, as she unwrapped the meat. Was the same thought occurring to Eric? Ten years ago he would never have forgotten to read a manuscript, certainly not Lise's. But then, ten years ago he'd been merely a professor.

"Maybe," Eric said quietly as he put the newspaper under his arm and started towards the den. "What time does your mother arrive?" he asked, turning back for a moment.

"Nine. I'll leave for the airport at eight. Can you manage with the history department? I'll be back in time to put out the food," Norah said, rinsing her hands under the tap. She was amazed at how much better she felt.

As the chops fried, Norah washed and peeled some vegetables. From where she stood in the kitchen, she could see that Eric had not sat down to read his paper. He stood at the den window, staring out at the three new trees he'd put in last weekend. Norah knew the apricot was in bad shape. She knew the man at the nursery had warned him that it was no time to put in apricots, but Eric had felt both confident and rebellious that day. Norah had helped him hold up the trees while he replaced the earth around their roots. He felt great tenderness for his trees. When he was done, he had asked her if it was so outrageous to rebel against the laws of nature, now and again. But Norah remembered feeling vaguely unsympathetic. It had been only an hour before the tree-planting that her mother had called, announcing her arrival the following week.

Norah cut up tomato into the salad. While her husband looked at his little trees, she knew his thoughts were not with their survival. She suspected that after having been reminded of Lise's manuscript, he had come home to search for it on his desk; his usual Friday afternoon frustration and exhaustion settling in. There had been a time once when work meant his own book. Work now meant budgets and salaries, meetings with the president and lunch with the provost. On his desk, he would find the usual confusion of papers and briefs, reports and letters. Lise's manuscript was in an orange folder at the back, under a pot of pencils. In the face of Eric's continual exhaustion, his even, steady nature was a source of wonderment to Norah. She knew this deanship was a step down, not up, for Eric. He had wanted more, much more. He would have preferred completing his book. He would rather have been inspired than an inspirer. But an inspirer he was. He still lowered the paper and looked over his lenses every morning as she breezed into the kitchen. Every morning it was a steady smile of approval regardless of all that had gone wrong in his life.

Norah suddenly felt embarrassed. She'd been awful at breakfast. From the moment she'd awakened she felt as though her head would explode. Nothing seemed to go right. While he had cracked into his soft-boiled egg, Eric had asked her what time her mother's flight got in. Not until that moment did she remember her mother's call of the weekend before. All he did was ask, and she had snapped at him over their morning coffee. Another sip, and then she had turned towards the window, thinking how relieved Eric must be that they hadn't planned to meet for lunch as they usually did on Fridays.

Norah stared at the salad she was preparing. He had ignored her snapping. He had wiped his mouth and glanced at his watch. She had known that he was meeting with the student demonstrators that morning, and in the afternoon, he had another budget committee meeting. He would handle it all. He always did, Norah had thought as she'd miserably left the house for work.

At the library she had muttered an inaudible 'good morning' to the night watchman who had just gone off duty. During the morning she'd had to deal with a junior high school tour and their inane teacher. At lunchtime she hadn't bothered going down for a drink; she ate her sandwich at her desk, alone, until Mr. Gantz appeared. Prematurely balding and cursed with halitosis, he stood there questioning her about that obscure reference having to do with *Pamela*. She had been most unhelpful. She had virtually ignored him, driven to distraction by his pot belly pressing up against her desk.

Then the girl, and Norah stupidly filing the reserve slip incorrectly. As if that weren't enough, there had been the business of walking over to her and staring, idiotically. She couldn't get over how uncomfortable she'd been, Norah thought, carrying the salad bowl to the table.

She stood for a moment at the window. It was almost dark. Fall leaves huddled along the white board fence. It really wasn't like her to be so at odds. She took pride in her work, caring for those books and making sure the art students' hands never left a smudge. When she wasn't doing her own research on the hand-illuminated musical manuscripts, she was continually cataloging the endless crumbling tomes for the collection. Even officious little things gave her great satisfaction; stamping books in, stamping books out, occasionally licking her fingers to speed through the tissue-thin pages of the huge reference books she kept piled on her desk. Norah turned back to the stove.

Later, when she'd stood at the cheese counter in the grocery store, trying to remember who taught in the history department, trying to recall their mates and whether they'd be Camembert people, or cheddar types, Norah drew a blank. Instead, she'd realized that her mother would arrive just in time to frown on her platter of cheese and salami. Norah shuddered. Had it really been so many years since that first time her mother had sat at their table, staring fiercely at an offending plate of butter next to the roast? She remembered reaching for Eric's hand under the table and then the three of them had sat there, uncomfortably, letting their dinner get cold. It had been many years and visits since, and still they never talked about things. Once off the plane, her mother would take off her suit and girdle. She would wobble in a loose, cotton housedress until she had to put on her girdle and suit again just before leaving for the airport. She would perch herself on the kitchen stool. Her still, thick legs in their beige, cotton stockings, dangling, as though they'd come apart from her torso if they weren't propped up by the black, tie-up shoes. Occasionally easing herself off the stool, she'd make herself another cup of tea with the bag she kept in a juice glass near the sink.

She should have followed her instinct and cancelled the history thing once she knew her mother was coming. But Eric had insisted, in his usual, calm manner, that there was no problem.

"You're still keeping yourself attractive, Norah," her mother would say all weekend, a combination of surprise and disapproval in her voice. "And how do you find time to keep busy in the kitchen?" she would ask, looking over at the corked bottles on the counter. "What is that stuff?"

Norah would tell her, and then she'd have to explain how she prepared it. She knew that her mother from the Bronx would suddenly want her recipe for tarragon vinegar, God knows why. She didn't tell her mother that year after year she filled those straw covered wine bottles with the vinegar, and every Christmas she gave it away to her co-librarians. Norah suddenly realized that because Toby was away at university this year, she would have to do all the wrapping and ribbon tying herself; not that she hadn't had to re-tie practically every ribbon her daughter had ever attempted. The annual Christmas wreath... somehow the fresh pine boughs, the red, taffeta ribbon and the small, copper bells, were inevitably tied into a disaster. Norah was always taking it off the front door after Toby had gone to bed, knowing that what she was doing was somehow very wrong. Nevertheless, she ironed the ribbon and did the whole thing over again. Of course, she wouldn't tell her mother that either.

Eric entered the kitchen with a bottle of liquor, heading towards the cupboard. Norah spooned the vegetables onto a platter and watched him take down the glasses. He poured from the bottle, added ice, and then slid the glasses under the tap for a second. Had he solved his dilemma about Lise's manuscript, Norah wondered? Or had he even considered it a dilemma? Possibly not. Could it be that he hadn't forgotten at all, and that he had intentionally not read it? Norah nodded as she reached for the glass that Eric handed her. She had heard him speak less and less about Lise's work. Each manuscript seemed to be read with more reluctance, until this last, which he hadn't read at all.

She watched him turn back to the den with his drink. Could it be that after all was said and done, Lise was not so extraordinary, not so unique? She would have liked that once, Norah thought, if Lise hadn't been so talented. But now she was older, and she really didn't care. If it were true though, that Lise wasn't so outstanding, it must be a very painful truth, Norah realized, glancing again at her husband.

When Lise was young and Eric not so young, when he had eagerly attended her youth from his mentor's stand, had he wanted more? Had he been content hoping to soak up the excess puddles of youth that waterlogged her feet? Was the girl's excitement, her rash, unswerving judgments, her searching, was it enough? While youth owns the world, age is merely part of it. Norah knew that now, but Eric, in his wisdom, must have known it all along. He must have wanted to protect Lise. It would be like Eric to want something like that, Norah thought. But whatever he wanted, it ended with bits of words and feelings, probably tiring, turning bitter inside him.

Afterwards, Lise moved to some place in the country where there was no running water, no electricity. Recently she came to town and dropped by to see Eric at his office. Eric had told Norah how startled he was to see Lise looking so exhausted, almost deranged. He had barely recognized her, he'd added sadly. It was as though she was grabbing out to middle-age, anxious to be rid of the follies and time-wasting of youth, eager to get on with life. She was completely obsessed with her work, Eric had said quietly.

Norah set out the plates and cutlery. Eric entered the kitchen and put his empty glass into the sink. Did he ever have regrets now, Norah wondered? Was he ever sorry that he hadn't gotten more involved? In Lise he had found a kindred spirit. Norah accepted that, and she realized that he had been searching all his life. Norah hoped he understood that she herself could never have been that soul mate.

"Norah, the visit with your mother will be just fine. You know that by now, don't you?" Eric's voice was gently teasing as he sat down at the table.

She carried over the platter of hot food.

"Norah?"

She looked up at her husband, completely confident that he was right.

"No problem, we'll take her to the new mall," Eric said, cutting into the meat. "Did you see Toby's letter? She seems quite happy with Botany 1, imagine that." Eric smiled over his plate.

Toby wrote? Norah hadn't even looked at the mail. Eric was an expert at re-building washed out bridges, and at raising laughter where it had been so long forgotten. Norah Banning knew that in a few hours she would rush eagerly to embrace her mother at the arrival gate. In a few hours, Eric would open the door to the first history people, cursing under his breath, not understanding why history could not have been combined with philosophy, or whatever, the week before.

THE SWIMMER FROM VANISHING POINT

When my younger sister Jacqueline asked if this year I would please take a cottage with her at Vanishing Point, our old childhood vacation spot, I surprised both of us by saying I'd think about it. I've never really done the beach, at least not as an adult. I'm not especially fond of the sun, not to mention all my other priorities, but I've never been forty-five either.

I'm Dora Maar, by the way. Need I tell you that our father, Pierre Bollet, who owned and operated a men's clothing store in London, Ontario, loved Picasso? He named the first three of us Dora Maar, Olga and Jacqueline. I inherited mother's restless, discontented soul and her Scottish genes; the height and red hair, fair skin and strong jaw. A far cry from my calm father, and Picasso's Dora Maar. When our mother, well pregnant for the fourth time, informed our short, adoring Quebecois father, that this was it, no more, he prayed for another girl. His prayer was answered, and he named the tiny, red, wrinkled infant, Marie Thérèse Françoise Fernande. Of course she was always Frannie to us. Free-spirited and pig-tailed, with a hint of pigeon toes and one lazy eye, a tom-boy, blessed with the names of three of Picasso's beautiful women. Naturally our names caused some discomfort in Anglo-Saxon, London, Ontario – where Bollet became Bowlit – and where of course, Picasso was neither viewed with awe, nor humor, in the Catholic parochial system that fate had thrust us upon. Nevertheless, we carried the names with pride and dignity, in deference to our father, despite the fact that they were legacies of misery, madness and suicide.

My husband Nate, hard working and conscientious, thinks the beach is a wonderful idea, although his instinct is to avoid the sun even more than I do. For him, August promises solid work, commuting back and forth from his Toronto architectural office to the firm's housing project for the elderly in Oshawa. But I deserve a break, he insists. Perhaps a little too eagerly? Nate, like all of us I suppose, is struggling with some form of mid-life crisis. Having recently become obsessed with his own mortality and lack of hedonistic pursuits, he had forced the Yuppies' R. & R. into his vocabulary. He's come to the conclusion that perhaps we should 'lighten up', to quote our Army Surplus attired daughters. He's quite right about a break. I've just finished editing another high school French book. He understands that in the last couple of years, things have seemed particularly bleak and pointless when I finish those textbooks; he understands the despondency, the restlessness. It wasn't always true of course. I used to enjoy my editing, especially when the girls were younger. My publisher used to say I was indispensable. Nate says our last child, our five-year old Ben – who waits patiently for his parents to have time – will love the beach.

We pack Jacqueline's station wagon on the 5th of August. Ben, and Jackie's Joshua, also five, as well as Joshua's two dachshund dogs, are beside themselves with excitement. They're already unpacking the bag of He-Man toys.

"Yesterday I went to Chinatown."

I throw the last bag of clothes into the back of the car, and glance up at Nate. "Chinatown?" He's standing beside the car, holding a package I haven't noticed before.

"I'm worried about the sun. You're not used to it." He unwraps a large, heavy, paper umbrella, covered with dragons and incredible blossoms.

"I wanted to get one of those spectacular bamboo helmets the rice pickers use, but I didn't think you'd wear it. I couldn't resist this!"

Despite his mother's early Alzheimer's, the relentless work to establish his firm, the tribulations of our twin daughters' rebellions, despite it all, bamboo and paper can still excite him, mid-life crisis or not.

"The guy said it'll keep off almost anything; sun, rain, snow!"

And thus, the moment of cold feet. The moment the whole idea strikes me as sheer stupidity. What business do I have going off to the beach? Never mind exhaustion and a five-year old son. There is other work to start. Why am I leaving my husband for three weeks? Isn't that what "The Seven Year Itch" was about? That goofy husband getting rid of his wife and kids for the summer, so he could play with Marilyn Monroe? Of course Nate isn't exactly goofy, I remind myself.

"Don't you like it?" He asks, opening and closing the umbrella. "I thought it'd be good for the sun."

"I love it, Nate." I run my hand over the fan folded paper.

We kiss good-bye, and he's leaning in through the car window, putting the umbrella into the back, beside the bag of beach toys.

Perhaps not goofy, but why is he so eager to get me off? I hate being forty-five. There are days when everything seems gray, saggy or suspicious. The house in Rosedale, the clothes in the closets; on occasion, my mind. Nate's face isn't gray or saggy. He's smiling, his arms resting on the window frame. He strokes my hair, mumbling something about relaxing, enjoying the water, that he'll miss me. His eyes are clear, upbeat; always receptive, always giving, despite the hurdles that life throws him. Yet I can't help thinking gray. At one end of the scale there are senile parents, and at the other, teenage children engulfing us, like algae in water, spreading, cutting off the air supply. When we free ourselves long enough to come up for a gasp, we find that it's precisely our patience that has worn down our crisp edges, and is turning us to moss. I'm not really worried about the Seven Year Itch stuff. We have a good marriage. I know we've been lucky really, compared to some of our friends. Lucky with the kids, our work, that we're still lovers. Does Nate think in saggy, gray patches? I suspect not. We kiss good-bye again. He's right, it's time for the beach. Nate reaches into the backseat to cuff Ben playfully, promising to come up for a weekend, at least.

After an hour of traffic, we meander through beautiful, leisurely farm country. Jackie insists on driving. I feel comfortably drowsy, and the boys and dogs are good. The radio is on; the sound of the local station hasn't changed. The swap shop still advertises old cellar windows and bushel baskets of sealers. The announcer still reads out recipes before the local news. '. . . beaches are open again for swimming after an accidental sewage spill further north . . . peaches from the Niagara fruit belt are expected on the market by next week . . . Crystal Dunn, from Seaforth, is still missing.' I lean my head against the back of the seat, wondering, briefly, who Crystal Dunn is.

Minutes later I'm pleasantly surprised to recognize landmarks in the landscape; the blue barn at the turn off to the lake route, a yellow brick farmhouse with a turret, another with a remarkable, gingerbread veranda. Jackie made all the arrangements for the cottage. As she drives, she recalls our grandmother's place; the long afternoons at the water, the spectacular sunsets. We reminisce about our father, how he'd remain in the city all week, tending the store. It gave him great satisfaction to know that his wife and daughters were at Vanishing Point, enjoying the sun and water, having a summer. On Saturday nights, he'd close up, and drive out to the beach for Sunday with his girls. I can still see our parents at the water. Mother had presence; her stature and flaming red hair, her confidence and carriage. She wore two piece, striped bathing suits, and she always looked beautiful. Her own mother had wanted her to go on the stage. She never did, she raised her girls instead, and rested. At the beach, on the lounger, she surrounded herself with umbrellas and straw hats, cold drinks, fruit, magazines and cigarettes. Whenever I get within sight of a lake, I smell her cocoa butter tanning lotion, her cigarettes. Breathless from running, we brought her iridescent sea shells and bits of quartz. She held them in her long fingers with the red nails, studying them intensely, as precious objects. Were there answers in those muted colors and bits of dancing light? Was her restlessness stilled? Father in the chair beside her – reading, his short, barrel build upright – brought mother certain comfort, peace. The water was clear and the sand white, and at night, large street lamps like the ones from the Paris métros lit the boardwalk the length of the beach. Our father had taken us all to Paris once – for Picasso of course – that's how we knew about the métros. Our parents are both dead now.

Jackie has turned off the highway and onto a blacktop side road. "Have you been to Vanishing Point recently?" I ask.

Jacqueline shakes her head, "I've been taking Joshua to Georgian Bay for the last few summers."

I nod. "Maybe the water – "

"Mom! Mom!"

I hear Ben scrambling forward in the back of the wagon.

"Just a minute Ben, let me finish," I pat his hand. "maybe the water's polluted and the sand is dirty," I suggest.

"Joshua has to pee! Joshua has to pee!" Ben's voice is behind my ear, he's tapping my arm with Skelator.

"Oh boy. Are you sure?" I ask, turning around.

Joshua nods urgently, pressing down on his jeans.

Jacqueline glances into the rear view mirror to catch sight of her son. "He's sure," she agrees, pulling off to the side of the road. "O.K. kid, let's go, out the back." She jumps out of the car, opens the rear door and leads Joshua down the grassy embankment. One dog starts to bark, the other remains asleep.

"This is your chance too, Ben."

"Don't have to." His face is pressed against the window, watching Joshua. "He always has trouble with his zippers," Ben mumbles.

In seconds, Jacqueline is climbing back into the front seat, and we're off again.

"Dirty sand and polluted water! Honestly, Dora Maar, you can be such a drag!" She laughs, her large, dark eyes sparkling. "I hope you're going to relax a little, Dora? Doesn't Nate ever tell you to?"

As a matter of fact, he does. But I won't admit that to my sister. My steady, responsible Nate. Despite his professional success, his seeming domestic content, now he wants change. Rather than appeal to my restless nature, this new development only makes me anxious. That's one reason I feel so uncomfortable with the idea of leaving him alone for three weeks. I hope this new R. & R. need doesn't involve something stupid, like buying a motorcycle, and insisting I ride with him. His mother would have had a coronary. Wouldn't another trip to Paris be just as satisfying? As for me, Nate's decided the nuns of my youth must surely have had something to do with the seriousness that doggedly accompanies me through life. Little does he know about growing up Catholic, or, London, Ontario.

"Did you hear me, Dora Maar?"

I turn to my sister.

"I hope you're going to relax, take it easy," Jacqueline repeats.

I nod, "Of course."

Jackie has sworn off men, at least for the summer. She's pretty, with straight, black hair and a slight face, but her breasts are awkwardly large for her slim body. She's only thirty-seven, so I figure she can afford to swear off men for a summer, especially given her track record. Little Joshua's father is history, so, for that matter, are Paul, Roger and Sean. As much as I love my sister, and vicariously enjoy her inevitably humorous, amorous escapades, I'm quite relieved that for three weeks I won't have to listen to her adventures.

The cottage is a small, frame structure squatting in the sand. When Jacqueline said she got it on the water, she wasn't kidding. It smells damp and closed inside, but it's adequately furnished, even sort of comfortable, with rattan arm chairs and a large coffee table. The counters in the kitchen have speckled, green formica, and there's a set of sticky tin canisters that have sea shells and small pebbles glued all over them. The crevices between shells and stones are filled with old flour and sugar, and something brownish that looks like molasses. I decide they've lost their charm, and whisk them under the kitchen sink before the boys see them and fall in love. Outside, the sand comes to the front door, and then inside a bit. The boys are already out beside the picture window, their He-Man collection and sand toys spread around them. Around the back, behind the house, the dachshunds are checking out the small wooded area infested with mosquitos and the last tenants' dog poop. A limp clothesline is strung between two pines.

If I get groceries, Jackie says she'll check out the waterfront with the boys. She's eager to rent some hand sailing equipment, and see if there might be swimming lessons. I unpack first, inspecting the bedrooms and bathroom. The dresser drawers have sand in them, and the bath tub is orange with rust stains. For some reason, the beeswax toilet seal is exposed above the linoleum floor. All kinds of odd things have become embedded. I suddenly remember why it is I don't 'do beaches', besides the sun, but I resolve not to let the cottage bother me. This is going to be a vacation. Later, after I return with groceries, Jackie has news of a pool, and that the boys are registered for a 9:00 a.m. beginners' class.

The next morning, in crisp air and a clear light, the boys and I walk along the empty beach to the lakeside pool. There's a small playground immediately beside the facility, with swings and slides and a fountain. The pier runs along behind it, jutting out into the water, congested with a large cargo boat and several small vessels. The town, with its Victorian houses, is up higher and inland, just a few minutes walk from the waterfront. Vanishing Point is so named because of that jutting bit of land along the shoreline that vanishes into the mist when seen from the water. After checking the boys in at the office and leading them to the change-room, I walk around to the front and find a place on the benches facing the pool.

Excitement and noise are at a high level. Mothers are chattering, babies in strollers suck pacifiers, demanding attention. I watch as Ben and Joshua are herded out of the change room, dripping from the obligatory shower, clinging to their towels. They're given a pep talk, and then told to slide into the pool, and hang on. Small children in front of me press against the link fence, calling out to siblings in the water.

Despite the chaos and confusion, I see him immediately. He enters the pool area and reaches for the life saving pole. An Athenian athlete readying for the games. For a few moments my eyes settle on him with rapt attention; I could be looking at the Parthenon, or the horses on the friezes, or perhaps a lone, Greek youth, rendered in marble. The profile is classical; nose, lips, chin. The hair, blond and curly. The definition of youth marks his body. The solid neck, an entity of its own, is separate from the line of the jaw, from the torso. He's a kid, a boy, surely no older than my twin daughters. He has an easy gait around the pool, a sweatshirt thrown over his shoulders, a naturalness with kids. Clearly he's one of the instructors. The other is a petite, well-hinged girl with a shrill, relentless voice. For half the lesson I watch attentively as Ben and Joshua struggle to master their fears. When I finally turn away for a moment, tired of the enervating sight, our eyes meet. In motion, he's like any eighteen-year-old boy with a remote, but nice look. But when still, not moving, his face becomes energized with an almost psychic sensitivity, the sky before the storm. This must be the power of the maharishi, of the guru. The wisdom, the pain, that beckons souls who follow blindly, riveting themselves to the halos of their leaders. But then he moves, and all is lost. Has he been watching me? Standing at the edge of the pool, his weight resting on his lifesaver's pole, he smiles at me. His partner shrieks out instructions to each child, flipping her head in the water like a porpoise, to remove the bangs from her eyes. There is sympathy in his glance, he understands my temporary anxiety over the boys' panic. I'm flattered. It's been a long time since I've been looked at like that.

As the days pass, I willingly wake up earlier than Jackie and take the kids for their lessons. We leave the cottage minutes before nine. I pad out across the sand with my coffee mug in hand, and take my place alongside the other mothers. I've gotten to know some of them. Pam is the one with the curlers in her hair. Debbie is a mother of twins, beautiful babies of nine months. With windbreakers zipped to our throats, we marvel at the children's bravery and spunk in the early morning cool. We speculate on the temperature for the day. We comment on the cleanliness of the pool and the pollution count of the beaches. There is discussion about which grocery store has the nicest produce and best pasta salad. I look forward to the early morning chatter; it leaves me free to observe, speculate and feel leisurely.

Occasionally there is talk of the male swimming instructor, who doubles as a lifeguard in the afternoons. It feels quite natural that there should be gossip – after all, the women talk of everything else. The boy lives alone somewhere as a boarder; they say he hates his father. Every morning he comes to the pool early, before anyone arrives, and does laps. They tell of how his own mother struggled with cancer and finally died last winter. How his father, an alcoholic child abuser, divorced her while she was ill, and remarried a woman with many children. I try not to pay much attention.

I find my reaction strange. I'm usually quite interested in trivia. But somehow I don't want to know about his daily life, his family, his girlfriend, which he surely must have. I prefer him nameless and abstract; a Heathcliff, Michelangelo's David, Christopher Plummer – the storm and the calm – the man, for whom environment is irrelevant. The man, for whom peace is not easy, and freedom, even in the form of resurrection, is what he unknowingly lives for.

Ben and Joshua like him. They talk about him all the time. At meals times, they chat happily about the things he can do underwater, as they pour ketchup on their hot dogs. For the most part, I ignore their talk.

"What are you after?" Jacqueline asks me one night, as we balance our glasses of wine and drag our loungers out over the sand to the edge of the water.

"Really, Dora, what?" She stands for a moment looking at me.

I'd forgotten that Jackie came with me one morning to watch the boys' lessons.

"I don't know." I dig my glass into the sand and settle back into the lounger.

"Maybe you want him?"

"Honestly, Jackie, doesn't bluntness ever get old for you?" I ask, tired out by the day in the water and sun.

"I'm serious, Dora, if that's what you want, go for it. Are you worried about Nate?"

"For God's sake!" I reach for my glass, sip the wine, and stare out across the dark lake. The smell of beach barbeques drifts towards us.

"Come on, TRUTH!"

"Jackie, the truth is, the lake is beautiful, the sky is dark and the sand is cool."

"Sure, but there are other truths, like your swimmer. I'll bet he's available. What do you think, Dora?"

The wine makes me feel lethargic, relaxed. Somehow I feel secure knowing the boys are asleep in the cottage, seeing the occasional spots of cottage lights dotting the shoreline, knowing that what I'm lying on is indeed a lounger, and not a boat. It would be nice though, to drift out onto the lake. Further along the shore is the famous Vanishing Point pushing out into the water, with two pines and a huge boulder. We used to go to it as children. I wonder if I could find my way back.

"You're not even going to talk about him, are you?"

I can hear the pout in my sister's voice. I turn my head, I see her profile in the dark. She's bored. We've been at the cottage for a week, and she's bored.

"They're still looking for that missing woman, Crystal Dunn, from Seaforth," I offer, reaching for my wine glass. "I heard on the news tonight that her family will give a reward for any information."

"Why won't you talk about him?"

"Jackie, there is nothing to talk about. This whole thing is beyond sex, I've tried to tell you that."

"Give me a break! Beyond sex! You're putting me off, and don't think I can't see through it. I know how you've been rushing off to get a glimpse of him every morning."

I ignore her.

"The boys' lessons?" Jacqueline adds.

"Shut up, Jackie."

"If I were you, I'd want him."

"Well you're not me. Thank God, because one of me is plenty." I feel angry and restless. I know it has nothing to do with Jackie.

The days drift on. In her boredom, Jackie abandons her vow to swear off men for the summer. Someone has caught her eye, and she begins spending serious time with him. I don't mind at all. I can watch the kids and dogs, and still read or think or daydream. In the afternoons, I follow them out across the warm sand, lawn chair in one arm, the paper umbrella in the other. I know I must cut quite a sight in Nate's shirt, my protection from the sun. Fortunately the boys are too young to notice or care what I wear in public. I speak with Nate every couple of nights. He tells me about work, and says I sound relaxed. I assure him I'm working on it. I don't tell him about the swimmer, and I don't ask what he does in the evenings. It's stupid, really.

"Joshua says he saw Portuguese-Men-of-War in the lake!" Ben is standing before me, taut, wide-eyed and dripping, pointing back to Joshua who has remained near the water.

"Really?" I shade my eyes and pretend to search the lake. "I can't see their boats. What color are they?"

"Mom!" His body eases, he shrieks with laughter. "They're not people! They're jellyfishes, with purple bags!"

"Oh yes, the jellyfishes. No dear, you tell your cousin that Lake Huron does not have Portuguese-Men-of-War."

"See!" Ben spins around, dashing off. "I told you! I told you!"

I watch them standing, facing each other, engrossed in conversation. Their arms wave, their heads turn, even their feet kick at sand. After a few moments they both shrug, and slide down to their castles. I'm amazed at their five-year old independence. Sand, water and sun seem to satisfy most of their needs. As for me, I find myself doing less and less everyday. Sometimes I spend whole, blank afternoons sitting and watching them play with the dogs. I realize I haven't once thought about the next editing job, or the bills I've left unpaid. Occasionally I think about the girls, wondering how their summer jobs are going, thinking I must call them. But when evening comes, I never remember. Days ago I gave up wanting to do anything. I haven't touched the needlepoint or knitting I brought. Sometimes hours pass before I even pick up the book I've taken out with me to the beach. I spend a great deal of time watching the sky through my glasses. I know about calm, summer days, and how the warmed earth's surface sends up thermals of air that rise, condense, and thus those flat-based, piled formations of water droplets. The low cumulus clouds drift and shift, their tops and sides illuminated by the sun. A sharpness of blue and white and detail, a softness of light. In the early evenings, after dinner, the boys and I walk to the Marina; a fishy breeze picks up around the boats, and we catch the late sun shattering like glass on the shore, where water meets rock.

The truth is, I've become obsessed with the swimmer. It's funny, isn't it? To think I was so worried about Nate getting itchy. Kindred spirits, soul mates, ships that pass in the night, call it what you will, there is an undeniable, silent, crashing of souls. I think about him teaching the lessons. I think about the day the boys and I arrived early, before anyone else. We sat on the bench and watched him doing laps; steady, long, driven laps. When he stopped for a few minutes to rest at the edge of the pool – unaware, I'm sure, of his audience

– he threw his head back and released a loud, almost violent laugh. He seemed distant, determined, surly.

I felt uncomfortable watching. And yet . . . I want to soothe him for the loss of his mother, though he has the power to self-heal. I grieve that he must live as a boarder, though his family exists. I probably want to make love with him, though he's the age of my daughters.

No words pass between us, until the day – it happens to be a Friday – that I decide our silence is ridiculous. I am a mature woman, I will speak, I will break the spell. As soon as the lesson is over, and while the boys dress, I stand up from the bench and walk towards the pool. Better still, I will pretend this is in my mind.

I stand at the link fence; my left arm raised, the fingers thrust through the wire. "How are the boys doing?" I'm pleased to hear my voice sounding mature, confident. I raise my free hand to my hair whipping in a sudden gust of wind. He moves toward the link fence, turning his sweatshirt right side out.

"Nicely, but they need more work with the backstroke. Could they put in some practice time in the afternoons?" He pulls on the shirt.

Is he relieved to break the silence? "Perhaps," I say, brushing hair out of my eyes.

His face is close to the wire mesh, to my fingers. I can hear him breathing, I can see the oil on his torso, but our words do not break the spell.

"It's going to be a beautiful day," he says suddenly, throwing his head back, staring straight above at the sky.

I nod in agreement, turning to look at the water. There are already sailboats out. Bathers are beginning to arrive with their beach paraphernalia. The vendors are preparing their carts.

"Meet me at Vanishing Point, tomorrow night at nine." His voice is a low, hoarse whisper.

For a strange moment, the clouds stop moving, I feel myself shifting into low gear. I look back at him, but it's an excruciatingly slow motion. His words seem to hang in the air, waiting for me. He's turned away; he's in motion, moving, bending in expectation towards a child, blue with cold and fear, clinging to the edge of the pool.

I blush. Smiling politely I turn around nervously, then hurry away. Walking back to the cottage with the boys, I can't help wondering if I've imagined what I heard. He couldn't possibly have said that.

"I dreamt last night." I tell Jackie the next morning, as I pour myself a cup of coffee. I slept fitfully, but dreamt fully and elaborately, not an unusual combination for me. It's Saturday, and the boys do not have swimming lessons. Fifteen minutes ago, they gulped down a bowl of cereal, and dashed outdoors.

"I never dream," Jacqueline says, carrying her coffee over to the rattan chair in front of the picture window.

She stares out at the water. I think her boyfriend has returned to the city.

"What are we going to do today?" she asks.

"I was on a beach, a long stretch of white sand."

"In your dream?"

I nod. "I came back to search for something I'd left behind. At first I didn't know what I was looking for, then I realized it was Frannie."

"Frannie? Our sister Frannie?" Jacqueline asks, amazed.

"Yes. Mother sent me back. She was very angry that I'd leave a small child alone near the water. I don't know how or why I did it, it seems pretty stupid now. But at the time it was crucial that I leave, there was some conflict in the dream, and it was very urgent that I go immediately, leaving Frannie. She was young, a small child. I had to walk along the shore for miles. I kept passing monument booths, like hot dog stands. You could wait while they made you a monument to order, a simple head stone, or a bust cast in bronze. They had all their foundry equipment behind the stands, half buried in sand. One place even carved in granite, to order. As samples of their work, they had an imitation of the Rosetta stone, and a huge postcard carved in the gray rock. It was from our Sister Olga to her boyfriend Jerzy, telling him it was best not to come to visit. They had done her signature beautifully. You know how nice Olga's signature is. The thing was almost as large as a billboard."

"I need more coffee," Jacqueline interrupts, standing up and walking across the raffia rug towards the kitchen. "I'd forgotten all about Jerzy.

What ever became of him?" she asks. "I was always sorry Olga didn't marry him. Why didn't mother like him?"

"Who knows. Mother didn't like a lot of our boyfriends. But about my dream. It was evening when I started back to find Frannie, I couldn't find anything. The monument stands were gone, everything was gone. It was as though there'd been a nuclear disaster; nothing was left, the sand had been raked clean. There was no sign of Frannie, except the plastic arm of her doll, sticking out of the sand."

"That was some dream. Did it end there?" Jacqueline asks.

"Yes, I woke myself up, I was terrified."

"So, what do you think, Dora? Are you going to abandon us, like you did Frannie?"

I look at my sister and laugh, but Jackie is serious.

"Listen I'll take the kids for a walk into town. Take a shower and get dressed, Jacqueline, maybe we ought to do something different today. It's Saturday, the beach will be impossible."

An hour later, when the kids and I get back, Jacqueline is sitting on the front stoop, painting her toe nails.

"Nate phoned!" She calls out, fanning her feet.

"He's coming! He'll be arriving late, around 9:00, and he'll be able to stay all Sunday. He said something about waiting up for him, so the two of you could take a walk to Vanishing Point."

In the afternoon, Jackie takes the boys on a picnic. When they return, I've swept the sand out of the cottage, baked two peach pies, and made a tray of roast chicken. When Nate arrives, I take him to sit out in the sand with a bottle of wine, instead of walking to Vanishing Point. I don't tell him about the swimmer.

Sunday is a rainy day. The first rainy day we've had since we've been here. Nate doesn't mind at all. He takes the boys for a walk along the beach in the rain, and then they play Monopoly, read comics and build a miniature cottage with small beach pebbles and Elmer's glue. I read, and stand at the window a lot, wondering if the swimmer went to Vanishing Point last night. Jacqueline looks through a Picasso book she's checked out of the public library. Jacqueline always thinks about our father on rainy days. It's a strangely quiet, calm day with Nate in the cottage.

That night Nate and I make delicious love, but I fall asleep thinking about the swimmer. I wonder if it's something similar for Nate.

Monday morning, and Nate leaves for Toronto at 6:00. I stand shivering in the cold air, still in my sleeping shirt. We kiss, and Nate says he'll try to get up some evening during our last week.

At ten to nine, we start out across the sand, towards the pool. The boys run ahead. I'm looking forward to the bench talk, the lesson, seeing him. The truth is, being near him makes me feel young. It really is as simple as that. For the moment, I don't care about anything else. I've never forgotten that picture of Dora Maar, standing in chest high water with Picasso. She was clearly beautiful, vibrant, sexy. All my life, I've tried to forget that Picasso's Dora Maar went mad.

"We don't have a lesson today!"

I look up to see Ben running towards me, twirling his towel in the air.

"What? Why not?"

"Don't know," he's still twirling, "something about the teacher."

"Stop!" I reach out to calm the towel, myself. My voice is anxious. "Where's Joshua?"

Ben turns and points toward a group of mothers standing beside the pool. Joshua is wedged in between Pam with the curlers and Debbie, the mother of twins. He's looking up at their faces, listening.

I hurry over to the women, glancing at the vacant pool. A 'NO LESSONS TODAY' sign is posted on the office door. "What's wrong?"

"It's the lifeguard," one woman volunteers.

"What?" I know my voice sounds high, clipped.

"He's in police custody."

"Police custody? Why? What happened?"

"They broke up a party late Saturday night. It was one of the kids' beer parties, they go on every weekend. It seems a woman claims the lifeguard attacked her, outside, behind the cottage. It's not clear what she was doing at a kids' party, apparently she's about forty. They say it was pretty messy, and she's sticking to her story."

A wave of nausea rises to my throat.

"Can you believe it!" Debbie says. "And to think," she lowers her voice, "to think he's with our children everyday. Our little girls!"

"No point in sticking around here." A young, nervous mother pulls away from the women, anxiously drawing a sweater over her shoulders, and turning to call her children.

"If you ask me," Pam adjusts the scarf over her curlers, "he probably had something to do with that Crystal Dunn woman from Seaforth."

All eyes turn towards her.

"Well, she disappeared didn't she?" Pam adds. "And clearly he likes older women."

Silence falls over the group.

"I guess it's possible," another voice says.

"More than possible!" Pam adds. "I'll bet anything they're going to find out he was involved."

"Do you think he – "

"I wouldn't be surprised to hear the worst."

"Don't you think we're letting our imaginations get the best of us?" I interrupt, weakly. But I'm ignored.

"How much do you want to bet they find her body down in an old well or something." Pam shakes her head, breathing deeply. "Maybe they'll get that crazy clairvoyant to help them. Any of you ever been up to Lamb's Way to visit with her? They say she'll read your palm for five bucks."

"Pam, stop it! You're scaring the kids!" Debbie says, nodding towards a cluster of wide eyed children.

Shock and loss sweep over me. Anger, and finally, stillness. It's several minutes before I pull myself together to call Ben and Joshua away from the playground.

Later in the afternoon, I start off down the beach towards Vanishing Point, alone. It takes a good half hour, the walk and the climb up the hill. By the time I get up, I'm shocked to see how changed it looks. The two pines are still there, but now the boulder is perched dangerously close to the edge of the cliff, or so it seems to me. I stand close and peer over at the rising lake that has eroded the cliffside, the precipice is frightening and steep.

"Shame, isn't it?"

I whirl around, my heart in my throat. An old man is standing between the pines, lighting a pipe. He's wearing blue jeans and suspenders but no shirt. His barrel build and bald head remind me of my father. Clearly he came up the other side of the hill. I must look surprised.

"Didn't mean to frighten you."

I shake my head.

"I say it's a shame the way the lake is eating up our land." He waves his pipe towards the cliff and the water. "Was a time when this was a beautiful spot. Won't be long before it might just vanish completely."

I nod, collecting myself. I shake some pine needles out of my sandals.

"I sure wouldn't want to be out here in the dark. That's a nasty precipice now!" He cackles, taking off down the other side of the hill.

I walk quickly, anxious to get back to the cottage. Nervous and uncomfortable, I feel the familiar crawl of prickly heat on my back, my physical response to anxiety. I want to see Ben and Joshua, Jackie, right away. I want to call the girls, I want to talk to Nate. I start to run, thinking of the time Nate and I were caught in a Paris subway during an accident. Before we realized what had happened, there was a loud, shrill alarm that wouldn't stop, and a crowd of anxious people gathered near a car door. A small child was screaming hysterically. Panic swept over me. The air was still and close and I was suddenly desperate to get out of the subway, to call home to Toronto, to make sure our children were safe and well. After several minutes of waiting, while time had stopped, a couple was led away by a subway attendant. The man was carrying a child, her hand bandaged in a bloody handkerchief.

I'm still running as I round the bend and the cottage comes into view. Ben and Joshua are playing in the sand. I stop to catch my breath, relieved, gasping, bending over, my hands on my waist. When I straighten up, I see the boys dashing towards me, laughing. After Sunday's rain, the landscape around them seems clear, clean. The sky looks promising. The tops and sides of my white, cumulus clouds are lit by the sun.

CONVERSATION IN THE LATE AFTERNOON

"My mother died when I was thirteen." The young man offered gently, sipping his wine, his voice velvet, smooth.

He sat on the couch to the left of Lera, Teddy on the right. His face was offensively ugly with over-sized teeth and lips; the body long and gangly.

"It's been downhill ever since – " He dropped his eyes to his enormous hands.

It was almost dark out; a silent dusk had fallen over the room. Lera glanced at Simon, her brother-in-law. He sat at the table, his hand and cigarette frozen at the end of his propped-up arm. He had his face turned to one side, a habit he favored when listening, but preferring to appear as though he wasn't. Had he stopped breathing? Not a muscle, not a hair moved. Yesterday they buried Simon's mother.

"Surely you don't mean that," Lera said, staring into the boy's face. "Wouldn't you like to re-word what you said?"

The boy looked at her uncertainly.

"Please Bob, it is Bob, isn't it?"

He nodded.

"Bob, please," she reached out and patted his hand – she must be drunk – "for all our sakes, please re-word your last statement." She knew Simon was waiting to breathe. Where had this clown come from? Lera wondered, trying to remember, focusing on the large hand she was patting. One minute she and Simon were fleeing his parental home – their less exhausted mates would deal with the people who whispered and hovered about Simon's father – fleeing to the quiet of Simon's house, where they could drink and talk. And the next minute, an old friend Teddy Campbell was at the door, to express his condolences. Bob, his 'significant other', had accompanied him.

"What I mean," Bob said, "is that everything changed after that. My life just wasn't the same."

"But actually down hill, as though your life was ruined or something?"

"Heavens no!" He laughed out, "is that what you thought?" He glanced from Lera to Teddy, then to Simon. "You see, it's just that I missed her terribly."

"Of course," Lera said.

"Well, thank God that's cleared up!" Simon said jokingly, rubbing out his cigarette butt. "On that note," he jumped up, "I think we should all have some more wine."

"I think I've had enough," Lera said, covering her glass.

"Nonsense, you haven't been so relaxed since this whole mess began."

"I agree with Simon!" Teddy said, leaning towards Lera. "I don't know what you've been like through this ordeal, but I don't remember ever seeing you quite like this!" He smiled.

"That's because you've never seen me drunk."

"Whatever, it suits you, and you haven't looked so well in years!"

"You should see me when I've had some sleep!"

Everyone chuckled politely.

"Was it horrid?" Teddy asked quietly.

Simon looked at him.

"I mean the funeral, was it wretched?"

"Ask Lera, she's the one who kept her head screwed on through it all," Simon answered.

If she'd kept her head screwed on, what the hell was she doing getting drunk the day after her mother-in-law's funeral, Lera vaguely wondered. For hours they'd been drinking and talking, getting progressively more ridiculous.

"Lera?"

She looked up from her wine.

"The funeral, was it more than you could bear?" Teddy asked again.

"The weather was so awful. Not that a beautiful, sunny day would have made any difference."

"No," Teddy agreed. "Although Mrs. Baron would have liked that." He smiled.

He had known Posey Baron well, Lera realized, far better than Posey had known him. For several years Teddy had house-sat for the Barons while they wintered in Florida. Posey had been pleased with him. Teddy was as clean and orderly as any fine lady could hope for.

Once, on a summer visit, Posey had called Lera into the guest bathroom, where she was cleaning, asking her if she had left cosmetics in the cabinet the last time she'd been to visit. Lera had assured her they weren't hers. She watched as Posey poked through the medicine cabinet, awed and amazed.

"Well then whose?" Posey asked, baffled.

"Probably Teddy's. No doubt he has extras, so he just left those here over the summer."

"Have you ever seen such a collection of stuff, Lera?" Posey shook her head, "I mean for a man, don't you think it's strange? Why would he want perfume and – look! Liquid make-up? If it's for his roles on the stage, you know, when he sings, then I could understand. But why would he have it here? Don't they usually put their make-up on at the theater?"

Lera nodded, "I think so."

"So why then?"

"So he can be pretty," Lera said, smiling.

"Lera, don't tease me, I'm perfectly serious. Why would a man want foundation cream and eyebrow pencils and eyeliner?" Her hand gingerly lifted things out, turned them around and upside down, and replaced them in the cabinet.

"I'm serious too, Posey. He wants to be pretty."

"Well I don't understand. Are you trying to tell me that Theodore is gay?"

Lera nodded.

Posey dropped her face to the sink and her cleaning rag. She was hurt, wounded. "But he seems like such a nice, sensible young man."

"He is."

"I really don't understand."

"Don't try."

Posey wiped out the sink and then turned to the counter. "Lera, tell me, what do they do?"

"Who?"

"Those men, you know, do they actually . . ." Posey lowered her voice to a whisper. "Do they embrace . . . ."

Lera nodded. "And then some."

"Oh for God's sake!" Posey said, suddenly indignant, losing any understanding she might have gained. Quickly she finished off the counter, replaced the toilet paper and kleenex, and left the bathroom.

Lera held out her wine glass towards Simon. "I think I'll have some more now."

Everyone clapped.

"You're quite right, Teddy. Mrs. Baron would have liked a sunny day." Lera agreed.

"WASN'T HEMINGWAY AT ENGHIEN?"

It BEGINS TO DRIZZLE shortly after they leave the hotel for their evening walk, so instead of having cognac and coffee out on the promenade – it's been their custom during this last week – they enter the *Pavillon du Lac Café*. Snuggled in at the curved windows that hang out over the water like a fish bowl, Claire Puig lightly taps at the glass. "Nira, there's our table!" She pauses, shakes her head, reconsiders. "Perhaps not the same table, but the very spot. Do you see, Nira? Imagine, more than sixty-five years ago my mother used to order *sorbets* for me!" Her voice animated, her cheeks slightly flushed from the walk, Claire leans forward in her chair, anxiously peering down through the dining room panes, down to the promenade. She hopes her chatter will distract the girl.

Nira momentarily turns away, struggling with the odd realization that every year there is less of her petite Gramclaire; less fabric, less flesh, less bone. She re-focuses on the pane of glass and her grandmother's tapping finger, on the white head. Only her hair remains unchanged – like her stubborn, Oise valley accent – wispy and white, rebellious and unruly as ever. Each evening her grandmother points out that table, and each evening she manages to propel herself back to the wistful expectations of her girlhood, her eager eyes still the color of summer, of bleached sand and blue water on a hazy afternoon. Nira is envious of the memories and pleasures of such eyes.

Claire sits back in her chair, comprehending her granddaughter's look. She sips her cognac and laughs. "Someday you'll have memories as fine as mine!"

Claire is grateful for Nira's smile. For a few moments she indulges herself with thoughts of her family. She permits fleeting, familiar glimpses of the deaths, the births, and the other milestones of her life to cross before her, until she manages to bring herself to the brink of satisfying tears. The very brink. She glances out across the lake. Now, at the age of seventy-five, Claire is quite willing to concede that she is, as her husband Julio always claims, 'an emotional animal.' Indeed she has the capacity for tears, at whim, but unlike Julio, for whom the sight of tears merely proves an annoying disruption, she considers them a source of energy, the yin and yang, and of course, she would never call herself sad, quite the contrary.

"It'll soon be dark, Nira," Claire says softly, her eyes still on the water, "and this is how I love it best."

Of course Claire knows that in the daytime, in the sun, the promenade above the lake is quite beautiful, with the mamas pushing strollers, and small children running along ahead, guiding balloons, or pulling tiny kites. So beautiful in fact, that it's hard to remember one's most serious preoccupations and obsessions. A relaxed, leisureliness descends on all who set foot onto the promenade, as though it's a strip of magic linking reality with dream. Outside the *Pavillon du Lac*, the café's swirling green and gold sandwich board sign – announcing the evening promenade orchestra – and its sparkling, multi-pane entrance, with the polished brass banisters and neat black trim, are still as much part of the landscape as the budding plane trees along the street reaching out over the walkway, as the Casino on the north shore, as the specks of white sails glistening on the water.

The promenade used to enthrall Claire, a child pulling up her white socks under the table, dabbing at her Sunday afternoon treat, bucking the breeze, and smoothing the hair out of her eyes. More than once she decided, firmly, it was really not that long, or that wide. As a matter of fact, it was possible to see the beginning and the end, even for a small child. And yet, when she was on it, it was as though it never ended, magically regenerating itself under her moving feet, for as long as she needed it.

As delightful as it is in daylight, Claire has always loved it best as it is now, in the early evenings. At this very moment, the patterned scallops and curls of the cast-iron railing stretch like a banner of black lace above the silver lake. The candelabra-shaped street lights along the railing appear at precise intervals of forty feet, their tall cast iron torsos atop cement pillars, sentinels above the water. The excitement is to wait patiently until that moment of dusk when they're illuminated, their three globes spilling a triangle of welcome light. The world of evening is ushered in, the mystery, the stillness, the sudden desire to stay out in the summer night air forever. On the far shore, rapidly darkening, the pine and cypress shake and yawn and curl in towards the small cottages sprinkled along the edge of the water.

"Then it really hasn't changed?" Nira asks, looking out over the landscape, wondering, briefly, if the casino functions year-round, and if the sailboats her grandmother talks about are out only during the summer months. According to the slim history she found in the hotel library, Enghien les Bains has been known as the "little Monte Carlo of the north," with its casino and racetrack. The thermal baths date from 1821. During the *Belle Epoque*, it experienced a resurgence of popularity, being the nearest spa to Paris. Sulphurous waters are prescribed for everything from chronic skin diseases to problems of the throat. Glancing intently at her watch, Nira briefly considers the possibility of sulphurous healing. A wonderful thought. One o'clock New York time. In a few hours her fellow students will protest the U.S. involvement in Nicaragua. It's the first time during the trip that she wishes she were home. Will it go smoothly? She worries about the tension; eager demonstrators, anxious administration.

"Changed? Not at all," Claire answers. She knows Nira isn't really interested in the landscape. It's the protest business at Columbia that has her activist granddaughter looking at her watch. Nira told her about it at breakfast; *café au lait*, *brioches*, and the *confiture de cérises* out on the veranda of their room, their patio chairs facing the pear orchards that stretch from the edge of the village into the valley. The air was crisp, and they sat wrapped in woolen blankets. Nira barely ate. But appetite or not, she spoke with conviction: nuclear arms and peace, women's advocacy, the Nicaraguan family her Crisis Center was sheltering. Afterwards, Nira fell back into an anxious moodiness that lasted all afternoon.

"Isn't it amazing!" Claire straightens up in her chair. "Sixty-five years, but the promenade, and the lake, the view, it's all the same." She looks at her granddaughter. Clearly there is something else. What is she to do with the girl? Recently Claire has had to listen to Julio spurting philosophy about the kinds of people who become committed to global issues. On the heels of his rantings, she's had to defend Nira and all those others. Julio has been irritable, unwilling. He feels left out. Claire is sympathetic. She understands how a creative life can sometimes rut the mind and isolate the soul until there is no tolerance left for group commitment. She sighs, thoughts of Julio weigh heavily. In any case, she does not believe the girl's preoccupation is entirely due to the Nicaraguan rebels or the Global Community.

"It's beautiful, isn't it?" Nira says, still staring out at the water, wondering how she can be so selfish, so preoccupied in the midst of such serenity? It would be naive to think that Gramclaire hasn't noticed. Naturally she has no intention of hurting her, but how will she ever broach this other matter? She has accompanied her grandmother from New York to France, vowing to tell her, vowing to make use of this time together and alone. For days she attempts to muster the wherewith-all. There is no one else in her family who can begin to understand, even begin! Only her Gramclaire. But she's old, it seems unfair to burden her. The shock could be devastating.

Claire nods. "For me, Enghien has always been one of the most wonderful places – *l'endoit plus sérène* – ." Their stay is almost over, but she has accomplished what she set out to do. Naturally a few days had to pass before she got over Julio not saying goodbye, but all was forgiven. They are both getting old, and she is not insensitive to his situation, to how difficult her absence must be for him. Claire nods thank you as the waiter brings their coffee. She desperately wanted to come back, and she wanted her twenty-one year old granddaughter to see the Oise Valley, Enghien. Of all her grandchildren, Nira is her favorite. She knows it's wrong, having favorites. With her own children of course, there was never a question of 'favorite.' But now that she's a generation removed, and seventy-five years old, can't she indulge herself? Of course she loves the others, that isn't the issue.

It's just that Nira is different – sensitive, eager – the only one who has ever expressed interest in her grandmother's past. The only one ever moved to tears by *La Marseillaise!* The others are prettier, far prettier, blond and healthy and American-looking. But Nira could be *Française*, with her slight build and the straight, brown hair, her impeccable accent. She has a thin, intense face, but lovely eyes, dark and intelligent. Her eyes will trap a man, when she's ready.

They have only two more days in Enghien, two more days of the lake, of the old *Hôtel des Bains* looking out over the Montmorency hills, of the peaceful village. Claire feels spunky and brave without Julio, almost as though she could embark on a new life. Perhaps if she were younger, she might try it. Like Nira, she too looked French once. Now, she's just an old lady, any old lady, for they're all the same, like babies. She does miss Julio, despite everything. She misses their evening hour sitting up in bed, drinking tea and talking. She even misses the dance company. He called early in the morning to apologize, to tell her she had been absolutely right about the business of doing something new for the piece. He assured her he's been working like an animal ever since she left. He's redone the entire second half, and the result is a magnificent piece of dance. Her husband does not suffer from modesty.

She was wrong not to have told him about her trip from the beginning, despite her concern over his reaction. Everyday she put off the momentous task, knowing what she would have to face. When she finally told him – only a week before her scheduled departure – it happened to be the very hour he came to her, asking for help.

"Not only that, but I've misplaced the notebook!" Julio Puig anxiously paces the kitchen floor. "Who would believe that Puig could forget how he choreographed Romeo and Juliet? It's unthinkable! My enemies would die laughing." He pauses at the table, a small, compact man, with a large, white mustache and tufts of snowy hair around his ears. One hand holds the back of his wife's chair, the other smoothes the shiny dome of his head. He does not smile, it is not amusing.

"Julio, it was years and years ago, why do you expect to remember?"

"I hate feeling old and stupid. Can't you help, Claire?" His voice softens as he appeals to his wife. "You know me, you've known me for over fifty years! Tell me what I would have done with the sequence in that *pas de deux*." Julio slides down onto the chair beside his wife. As he hums a few bars of the perplexing music, he reaches for the stubby, colored glass salt shaker and holds it up squinting, to the light of the window.

Claire knows this is an old habit, something he does when he's at a loss.

"You know the sequence I'm talking about?"

Claire nods.

"So tell me Claire, what would I have done?"

"Perhaps it wasn't meant to be remembered," Claire says gently, knowing her words will anger her husband. She slips the needle in and out of the aqua tulle. The white cat, Adagio, purrs at her feet.

"What's that mean?" Julio cocks his head suspiciously, the shaker suspended in the rays of light.

"Could Prokofiev be wanting something new from you, Julio?" She ventures, looking at him intently, her fingers smooth the garment as she works.

"Insults, from you!" Julio barks, bringing down the shaker, jumping to his feet. "You, of all people? I'm surrounded by chaos and confusion, and now insults! Do you think I have time to waste!" He begins to pace again. "I'm getting old Claire, old! I can't have many years left. Besides, since when do you know anything about choreography? Tell me, since when?"

Claire bites off the thread and calmly slips the needle into the top of her apron. "I must be mistaken. I've always considered you a creator, whether young, or old with little time." She stands, pulling herself up to her full height as she gently shakes out the leotard with tulle sewn around the hips.

"Finished?"

Claire nods, folding the costume, placing it on the ironing board.

"I love you Claire." Julio whispers softly, moving in silently.

She remains standing at the ironing board, her back to him. He places his hands on her hips; he bends to kiss the nape of her neck.

"You always insult me." She closes her eyes. "No more!" She pulls away.

Julio drops his head sheepishly as he stoops to pick up Adagio. "But I'm not doing anything I haven't done for fifty years!" He strokes the white fur.

"I want you to stop insulting me."

"Claire, you're used to it. Besides, I talk too much. It doesn't mean anything, you know that."

"How dare you say it doesn't mean anything?" Claire turns and faces her husband, her voice shaking, her eyes moist and vulnerable. She breathes deeply, slowly, gathering her forces. "I just turned seventy-five, and I've had enough, too many put-downs, too much humiliation – " she pauses, "I have something to tell you Julio."

Julio makes a face and lets the cat go. "Haven't you finished?" His voice is cold, matter-of-fact.

Claire knows that when her husband feels cornered, he attacks before being attacked.

"I came in here to get your advice, not a lecture. I've called a rehearsal for Wednesday and I must resolve this problem. This is not a small matter, Claire."

"Nor is this," Claire says quietly, staring at the window over the table. "I'm going away." She watches as Adagio, sitting beside the geranium, talks through the glass to the neighborhood tom.

"Would you stop interrupting – " Julio blurts.

"Listen to me Julio," Claire turns back, her voice controlled, "I'm going on a trip, in a week. I'm leaving. I've arranged for Mrs. Manfred to come in and cook for you."

"What are you talking about Claire, leaving and trips, Mrs. Manfred!" Confused, Julio waves his arms impatiently above his head.

"I'm going back to Enghien."

"Enghien? I thought we decided to put off France until next spring."

"You decided, not me."

Julio delights in abusing her village, spurting that it's lethargic, decadent. Of course he does the same with Barcelona, and he was born there. 'They're the old countries,' he's always reprimanding her, 'and we're Americans.' Not that he doesn't enjoy being known as a Spaniard, a stubborn, Catalan choreographer. Not that he doesn't enjoy bursting out to his dancers in Spanish – furious, impatient shouts, or thick, mellow praises. "I told you I wanted to go back to Enghien, I haven't been back in over ten years, not since my mother died. I told you that in December. I said if you weren't coming, I would go without you. That was three months ago."

"But you've never gone on a trip without me!"

"I know, but I'm getting old, just like you are, and I want to see Enghien again before I die. That's all, it's not very complicated."

"Don't be silly, Claire. What will you do in Enghien? It's a village, nothing!"

"The same thing I've always done in Enghien," Claire says simply.

"But we haven't even talked about it!"

"There's nothing to talk about Julio. I'm taking Nira with me."

"Nira? What would she want with Enghien?"

Julio too had claimed Nira, years ago, when she was a child.

"It's spring break, so she won't miss any classes. Graduation is in June. This will be my present. Besides, I think she needs to get away for a while."

"What's wrong?"

"Nothing is wrong, I just sense she's tired, tired of school and studying."

"There's nothing wrong with her that a lover couldn't cure. Why doesn't she have one anyway?"

"Perhaps she does. Besides, since when do you know what a lover can or can't cure?"

"But Claire," Julio's voice pleads, "you can't be serious. How can you do this, just when I'm going to start rehearsals? Besides, I hate to see Mrs. Manfred wobbling around. And how do you know she can cook?"

"She can cook. Just don't look at her," Claire offers.

"Who will finish the costumes?"

"Betty, *la fillette*, who helped us with the Rite of Spring wardrobe last year. She can do it all. It's not very complicated, sewing tulle skirts onto leotards. I know, I've been doing it all my life."

"What are you thinking about, Gramclaire?"

Claire turns; Nira hasn't called her that in years. She watches her granddaughter building a fortress with the sugar cubes. She seems calmer. "Your grandfather."

"What else did he say this morning? He's been working like an animal, right?" Nira smiles. She knows her grandmother was wounded by his refusal to say goodbye, to wish her a good trip. As the cab pulled away from their brownstone, Claire burst into tears. 'Is he still standing on the step? Nira look, is he still there? I don't want him to see me turn around!' During the ride out to Kennedy, Claire fussed nervously in the back seat, arranging and rearranging herself and her belongings. Nira had never seen her grandmother so flustered and anxious, fluctuating from anger at his stubborn, selfish behavior, to weeping and guilt and second thoughts about her journey. Nira tried to calm her, but Claire would not be consoled. At one point she even insisted the cabbie immediately turn around and go back! It was several hours before most of Claire's anger dissipated.

"Yes, working like an animal, as usual," Claire says, adding sugar to her coffee.

Nira's grandfather always said that in the context of hard work. When she was little she used to sit in the corner of the dance floor and watch while he taught his classes. She had no trouble visualizing him as an animal, hard at work. He always appeared as some unknown creature, a cross between a rabbit and a burro. Upright, fuzzy, and in ballet slippers, his ears alert as one front paw adjusted his glasses. Explaining an intricate series of movements to the dancers, or perhaps mincing easily across the floor, his tail would be modestly tucked into his sweatpants.

"And he said he loves me," Claire smiles. It still amazes her that she actually talked to him about "put downs" and "humiliation." She's never done that, she's never even dreamt she was capable of it.

"Of course he loves you Gramclaire," Nira says gently, replacing all the sugar cubes back in the bowl.

"Why 'of course?' When two old people fight, Nira, the resilience of youth is gone, there just isn't as much love left to make up with."

Still so feisty, her old Gramclaire. Nira realizes that for the first time in days, she finds herself relaxing. Infinitely grateful for the bit of peace, she actually feels positive, as though she might even take on the world again. It's good. She watches as a waiter ushers a middle-aged couple over to a nearby table. The man exchanges a few words with the waiter, indicating they are foreigners, tourists from Germany.

Afterwards, the waiter turns to Claire and Nira's table, and Claire orders more coffee.

"Do you want another *palmier*, Nira?"

Nira shakes her head, and the waiter leaves. There are wonderful moments of silence. She watches as her grandmother carefully adjusts the scarf around her neck, her eyes, her face, lost in thought.

"I'm very sorry you never knew your grand uncle Raoul!" Claire's voice is sudden and energetic. A swift yearning for the richly layered years of her childhood inexplicably sweeps over her. "He used to paint that scene," she smiles, waving to the lake and the promenade. "Sometimes he'd go around to the back of the hotel, and paint the valley and le *petit village* in the distance. The owner of the hotel let him work up in an attic room that had a window looking out over the landscape. Raoul had to give him every fifth painting, and the owner hung them in the dining room."

"Was he a good painter?" Nira asks.

"Good, but not great. Raoul worked hard, and eventually he moved to a studio in Paris. Sometimes when he came home to visit, he'd paint down at the promenade, the third lamp post in from the far end. I used to watch him for hours. I'd stand at his elbow, watching every movement of his wrist, every dab of the brush, every squint of his eye. When he finished a tube of paint, he would reach in his pocket for money, and send me to the little store in the *centre ville* for more. I adored it, I used to wait for the moment he ran out of paint."

"What did your mother think?"

"She was convinced Raoul was a genius, and nothing should get in his way. It was our duty as women to facilitate things for him. He was only to preoccupy himself with his *oeuvre*."

"Didn't it bother you to be at his beck and call?"

"No. But sometimes I wished I could try it," Claire says quietly.

"Try what?"

"Holding a brush in my hand, knowing what it feels like, to put paint on a canvas."

"Why didn't you ever do it, Gramclaire?"

Claire shrugs. "Too busy, I guess. You know, the children, the house, and when there was extra time, your grandfather needed me for the costumes." She wonders how many times Julio picks up the colored glass shaker in her absence? How many times does he hold it up to the sunlight, hoping those prisms will ignite his brain? Does he wish for her return, really wish for it? Is the quality of his life less, without her? "Things were different then. A woman wasn't a free agent, the way you girls are now. We were always there for someone, first our parents and brothers, then our husbands. It was another time. You come and go, your parents think nothing of letting you move about alone in your own world. You make your own decisions and choices. Life is as open to you as to men." She misses her husband, and yes, the quality of her life is not the same.

Nira watches her grandmother's face as she speaks. She wonders if her generous Gramclaire has the vaguest notion of how open life is now. Gaping is a better word. She's always admired her grandmother's indomitable spirit, despite her husband's oppression, her children's needs. But now, how will this old lady deal with her favorite grandchild's predicament? Will the generosity remain? Will the gentleness and wisdom guide? Because her grandmother is the most loving, the most realistic of all her family, Nira is about to make her suffer.

"What's wrong Nira?"

"What?"

"Are you going to tell me about it? I don't believe it's just the rally."

"Why not?"

"There's more than rally in your eyes."

Nira smiles.

"Your courses are almost over aren't they?"

"Yes, a couple more months."

"And you have a job waiting for you at the publishing house?"

Nira nods.

"So it must be your love life."

Nira blushes.

"Your grandfather has been asking me why you don't have a lover. I told him that maybe you do. Am I right?"

"Yes."

"Wonderful. Your parents know?"

"Not everything."

"Have they met at least?"

"Not yet."

"You must introduce them. Parents are happy when their children are happy."

"I don't think they'll understand."

"Trust them."

"My lover is a woman." Nira finishes off her coffee and then – as though changing the subject, as though desiring to shift the weight of her personal burden – she points out the windows towards the distant fields beyond the lake. "Wasn't Hemingway here, in the twenties?" Once again, Nira is overwhelmed with pain. "I read once that he'd drive up with Gertrude Stein and Toklas, picnicking on the way and stopping at the racetracks?" She waits.

"Gramclaire?"

Claire remains quite still, only her head nodding in its barely perceptible manner of stress.

"I'm sorry, Gramclaire. You can't imagine how sorry I am. I've even considered the thermal baths, hoping for a cure!"

A gasp, followed by a laugh, breaks Claire's silence. She surprises herself. For several seconds she looks at her granddaughter's anxious face. Then, "Hemingway certainly was here. You know that I met him? I was just a girl, maybe fifteen." Claire suddenly sits up very straight, her head erect, her eyes shining, "and I found him very handsome, *vraiment très beau*. It was here, here on the promenade, I was with Mama and Raoul. We were finishing our walk when Raoul spotted him. Naturally they had met in Paris. Didn't I tell you that Raoul had many friends? Well you see – " Claire reaches up to her eyes with one hand, quickly, as though she's used to wiping away her tears before they're noticed, before they become an issue, "you see your grand uncle Raoul was very popular. Enghien, Paris, wherever he went. But about Hemingway – " Claire pauses and looks down at the table. Her granddaughter's young hand is covering hers, shielding, protecting. Claire brings down her other hand and gently embraces Nira's. "You know that he had incredible presence, a magnetism really, yes, we were just finishing our walk, it had been such *beau temps*, such a beautiful afternoon – "

Claire hopes to distract the girl with her chatter.

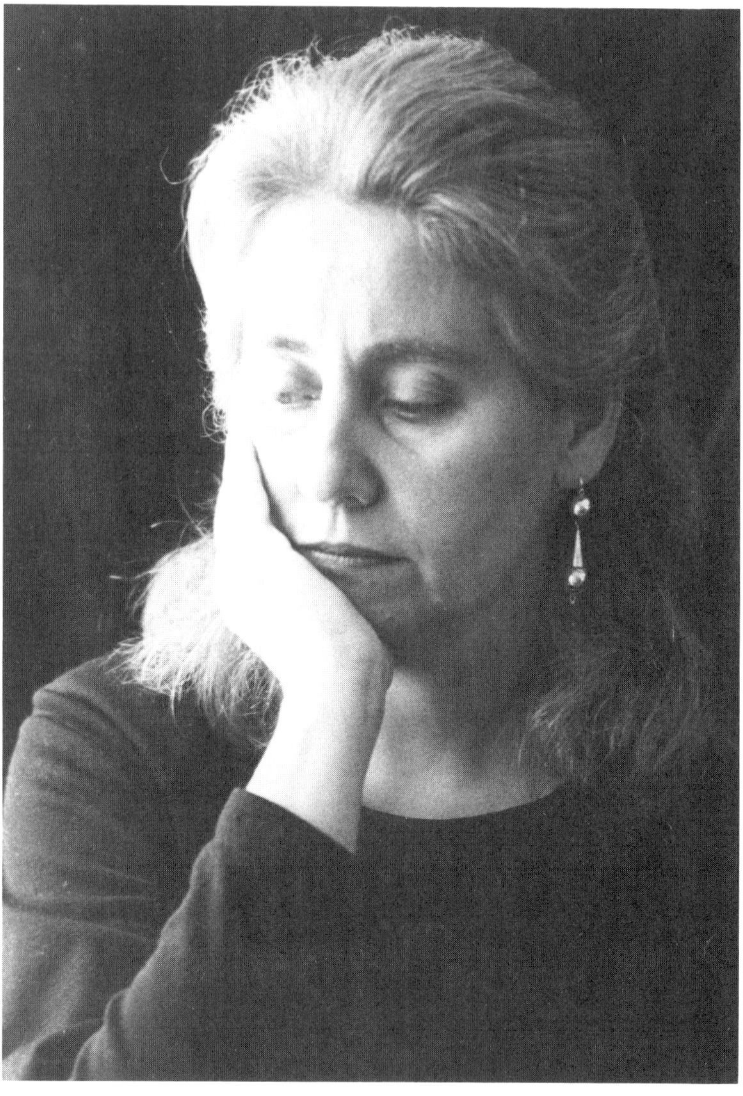

NINA BARRAGAN

the pen name of Rocío Lasansky Weinstein, was born in Cordoba, Argentina. She was raised and educated in Iowa City, Iowa, where she now lives with her husband, artist Alan Weinstein, and their four children. She has traveled extensively, with residencies in Ibiza, Spain, Bergen-am-Zee, Holland, Regina, Saskatchewan, and Teeswater, Ontario. Currently, she and her husband are co-partners of The Barn Collections, an art gallery.

"I have never had a time without writing: it is my window to the world. I observe through it and project through it, hoping to reach others, hoping to ease the chaos of loneliness and uncertainty. Writing has always kept me complete, and its persistent tapping is central to my life," Barragan says, adding "my life includes baking, laundry, nurturing my family, and of course, just observing."

She collaborated with her husband on *The Egyptian Man*, a limited edition, large format, fine art book, and has also been published under the name of Emily Hollis McIver. *No Peace at Versailles* is her first collection of stories.